PAINTED PONIES

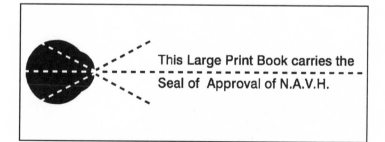

This Large Print Book carries the
Seal of Approval of N.A.V.H.

PAINTED PONIES

AMANDA HARTE

THORNDIKE PRESS

A part of Gale, Cengage Learning

GALE
CENGAGE Learning·

Detroit • New York • San Francisco • New Haven, Conn • Waterville, Maine • London

GALE
CENGAGE Learning™

Copyright © 2006 by Christine B. Tayntor.
A Hidden Falls Romance Series #1.
Thorndike Press, a part of Gale, Cengage Learning.

LIBRARY OF CONGRESS CATALOGING-IN-PUBLICATION DATA

Harte, Amanda.
    Painted ponies / by Amanda Harte.
      p. cm. — (Thorndike Press large print clean reads) (A
    hidden falls romance series : no. 1)
    ISBN-13: 978-1-4104-1396-3 (alk. paper)
    ISBN-10: 1-4104-1396-9 (alk. paper)
    1. Disfigured persons—Fiction. 2. Twins—Fiction. 3. Large
type books. I. Title.
PS3515.A79457P35 2009
813'.6—dc22
                                     2008055962

Published in 2009 by arrangement with Thomas Bouregy & Co., Inc.

For Karen Ann Kish, whose friendship helped me through a difficult time. Thanks, Karen, for reminding me how important it is to believe in (and create) happy endings.

CHAPTER ONE

August, 1908

Homecomings were supposed to be happy occasions. Anne Moreland forced her lips to curve upward, hoping no one would notice that the smile was a sham, as false as the rest of her face. Jane would know, but Jane, Anne saw as she glanced at the woman next to her, was staring out the window, the reflection in the virtually spotless glass revealing a smile that bordered on a grin. At least one of the Moreland twins was glad to be returning to Hidden Falls.

As the whistle blew and the train shuddered to a stop, Anne rose. There was no point in delaying. She had seen the speculative look the conductor had given her when he'd taken their tickets and the way he'd averted his eyes. Perhaps she should have left the veil covering her face, but a veil, Anne knew, would only have postponed the inevitable, which was why she had draped it back over her hat. She was home, for better or for worse. Anne winced at her poor choice of words. Marriage vows were most assuredly not part of her future.

"Where do you suppose he is?" Anne turned toward her sister as they reached the bottom of the iron steps. The arrival of the afternoon train was a routine event, no longer heralded with the fanfare that had marked the first year of its existence. Families seldom came to the station to watch the great iron horse that carried supplies to the Moreland Mills and transported the finished textiles to markets in New York City and beyond. Now the only people who lined the platform were those who waited for passengers or a special delivery. There were no more than half a dozen of them, and he wasn't one of them.

"Who?" Jane sounded distracted, though it was clear that she, too, was searching the train platform. Something, perhaps the heat that was unseasonable even for August, had brought a flush to Jane's cheeks. Her own, Anne knew, were paler than normal, and she clenched her teeth to keep them from chattering. That had nothing to do with the weather and everything to do with the face she scarcely recognized.

"Why, Charles, of course. Who else would

be meeting us?"

Jane nodded. "Of course, Charles." If she hadn't known better, Anne might have thought that Jane was looking for someone other than their brother, but that was silly. No one else knew that they were to arrive on today's train. It was Charles who was to meet them and Charles who obviously hadn't come. The porters had deposited their trunks at the edge of the platform while the other passengers dispersed. There was no one left at the station, and Bridge Street was empty, save for the wagon that was crossing the river at a foolhardy speed. Although it had come down the hill from the direction of Fairlawn, Anne didn't recognize either the wagon or the driver.

"Oh, my!"

Though she didn't voice the words, Anne's thoughts echoed her sister's exclamation. The man who leapt from the wagon and hurried toward them was the most handsome creature Anne had ever seen. As tall as her brother, this man's hair was golden rather than the sandy blond all the Moreland children had inherited from their mother. She imagined that his eyes were blue like theirs — it was impossible to tell at this distance — but that was where the similarity ended. His face was angular with

9

a strong, straight nose that might have overpowered anyone else. On him, it appeared perfect, as did the faint cleft in his chin. Tiny lines bracketed his mouth, adding to the impression of strength — and beauty. Though Anne knew that men were not normally described as beautiful, that was the only adjective that suited this man.

"Miss Moreland?" The man doffed his hat in greeting. His voice was low and mellow, giving no hint that he'd just sprinted from the wagon to the train platform, though the stock that he wore in lieu of a collar appeared to have been hastily tied.

Anne nodded. "We're both Miss Moreland." She gestured toward the woman who stood next to her, Jane's bemused expression telling Anne that she was as startled by the man's appearance as Anne herself. "This is my sister Jane, and I'm . . ."

"Anne." Though the man glanced at Jane, he smiled at Anne, and she saw that his eyes were indeed the blue she had expected. What she hadn't expected was the fact that they tilted up ever so slightly at the edges, giving him a faintly exotic appearance. She couldn't have anticipated that or that there would be something in his expression that she couldn't identify. Pity. Of course it was pity. By now she ought to be accustomed to that.

"I'm Rob Ludlow," he said. "I apologize for my tardiness. One of the wagon wheels was loose."

As Anne started to nod her understanding, Jane took a step forward. "Where's Charles? Don't tell me there's another problem at the mill." The sharpness in Jane's voice startled Anne.

Rob Ludlow appeared not to notice Jane's annoyance or the fact that she continued to look behind him, as if she expected someone else to appear. He gestured to one of the porters to load the pile of trunks into the back of the wagon. "The mill is running smoothly," he said, offering an arm to each of the sisters as he escorted them from the platform. "It's merely that we didn't expect you to return for another few weeks. Your brother thought he would be back by then."

Anne's step faltered. Though she knew she had changed, she had expected her home to be the same. She had thought that she and Jane and Charles would once again be a family. But that, it appeared, would not happen, at least not today.

"Back? Where has Charles gone?" The words tumbled out before Anne could stop them. It wasn't like her brother to leave

Hidden Falls, particularly not after the series of problems that had plagued the mill over the past year. Though he had made light of them in his letters, Anne had realized that he worried about the mill, just as he would worry about her when he learned of her plans. The only good thing she could find in his absence was that she had a reprieve.

"Charles is in Paris." A grin crossed Rob's face, and — although Anne hadn't thought it possible — it only added to his beauty. "If I'm not mistaken, he's hoping to return with a bride."

Another change. Had nothing remained the same? Still, this one might be good. Though Anne's lips started to curve at the thought that someone in the family would be happy, her sister's words caused the smile to fade. "Who are you?" Jane demanded of Rob. She took her hand off his arm and turned to face him, her stance openly defiant. "Are you running the mill in Charles's absence?"

Anne stared at the woman who used to be her identical twin. It wasn't like Jane to be so shrewish. If anything, she had been the happier sister. Perhaps the strain of the last year was taking its toll on her. As the porters loaded the last of the trunks into the wagon,

Anne reached for the tip that she'd in her pocket. The sooner she and reached Fairlawn, the better. They'd already provided enough grist for the town's rumor mill.

Apparently unconcerned by Jane's hostility, Rob shook his head. "I'm afraid that I know nothing about operating a mill. Fortunately, that wasn't what Charles asked me to do." A hint of a deprecating smile teased the corners of Rob's mouth. Anne found herself staring at him, wondering why he seemed familiar, when she was certain she had never met Rob Ludlow.

Rob shrugged, as what he was going to say was of little importance. "Your brother hired me to do some woodworking."

As Anne glanced at his gloved hands, she wondered if they bore cuts and traces of paint. Charles had said nothing about carpentry work, but he also hadn't admitted that he was contemplating marriage. What other surprises were waiting for her?

When both women were seated in the wagon, Rob flicked the reins, and the horses began to move at a sedate pace, crossing the river to climb the hill to what the townspeople called Rich Man's Row. As they passed the first house, Anne saw that one of Henry Ford's Model Ts was parked

: drive. Jane's lips thinned with
ispleasure, making Anne wonder
rad Harrod Jane had been look-
id she expected him to meet them
n station, and was his absence the
reason she had been so uncharacteristically
curt? A year ago, Jane had been a frequent
passenger in their neighbor's automobile,
and there had been speculation that Brad
would ask for Jane's hand in marriage,
perhaps the night of his parents' anniversary
party. But that had been the night that . . .

Anne turned toward Rob and the river,
refusing to think about that night, refusing
to look at the soot-covered bricks of the next
house, the one that she called home. "Thank
you for coming to meet us," she said to Rob,
her head resolutely averted from the shell
that had been her parents' wing.

Rob slowed the horses as they entered
Fairlawn's curving drive. It was still a
beautiful house, if you didn't look at the
south wing. Though Charles had once called
the castle-like crenellations pretentious,
Anne had always loved the building. "Papa
said that Jane and I are the Moreland
princesses," she had told her brother. "That
means that we have to live in a castle."
Charles had merely laughed and ruffled her
hair. They'd been a family that day. Now . . .

Anne fixed her attention on the man who sat next to her. "Thank you, Mr. Ludlow," she repeated.

"It was my pleasure." Though the reply could have been nothing more than a polite answer, Rob seemed to mean it, and his smile helped dispel Anne's gloomy thoughts. Seconds later they reached the front portico. Anne and Jane were home.

"Oh, lambies!" A gray-haired woman held out her arms as the sisters descended from the wagon. Mrs. Enke, Anne saw, had not changed. She still wore her hair in a coronet of braids that had been out of style for more years than Anne had been alive. She still wore dresses of unrelieved black with sensible black boots. And she still greeted Anne and Jane with more enthusiasm than anyone other than their mother.

"Let me take a look at you." The Morelands' housekeeper gave Anne a hug, then held her at arm's length. Squinting, she announced. "More beautiful than ever." It was a lie, Anne knew, but coming from Mrs. Enke, it didn't hurt the way the train conductor's scrutiny had. "I thank my lucky stars you're home again. This house needs more women." She shooed Anne and her sister up the brick steps, much as she had when they were children, adding, "I made that cinnamon shortbread you always liked. You come right in here and set yourselves down. I'll have some for you in a jiffy." Mrs. Enke opened the door to the front parlor, the room where Anne's mother had once entertained her neighbors.

Jane hesitated in the doorway. "I'm sorry, Mrs. Enke, but I'm more tired than I realized. I think I'll rest a bit."

Anne gave her sister an appraising look. Jane's face was flushed, perhaps from fatigue, perhaps from an incipient illness. "Do you want me to go upstairs with you?" As Jane shook her head, Anne turned toward the housekeeper. "I've missed your cinnamon shortbread," she said truthfully. Though Charles would have scoffed, there had been days when Anne had held a cinnamon pomander to her nose, telling herself that the pain would fade and that soon she would be back in Hidden Falls, drinking a cup of Mrs. Enke's hot chocolate and savoring a piece of cinnamon shortbread. It was too warm for cocoa today, but the delicious aroma of cinnamon filled the house, reminding Anne of happier times. "There was nothing like it in Switzerland."

Mrs. Enke nodded, as if she knew that Swiss pastries, no matter how delicious they were reputed to be, could not compare to her baking. Minutes later, she returned, carrying a tray. "Oh, lambie. It's so good to have you back." The housekeeper laid the tray on the table in front of Anne. "Men just don't appreciate things. Why, your brother lets those two filthy dogs of his sleep in the house." Mrs. Enke poured a cup of tea, adding the dash of milk that she knew Anne preferred. "I ask you, who is supposed to clean up after them?"

Anne took a sip of tea to hide her smile. She had read between the lines in Charles's letters and realized that he and Mrs. Enke had disagreed on a number of things, not the least of which was the presence of puppies at Fairlawn. "Where are Salt and Pepper?" she asked. There had been no sign of animals when they'd approached the house, and the parlor bore no traces of fur.

"That foolish man took them with him all the way to Paris, France, and if the good Lord answers my prayers, he won't bring them back."

Anne bit into a piece of shortbread, savoring the delicate flavor. "This is delicious. I can't count the number of times I wished for a piece of your shortbread." Though it was nothing less than the truth, Anne hoped Mrs. Enke would accept the change of subject.

"I knew you'd appreciate it, lambie." The respite was brief, for the housekeeper frowned as she continued. "You always were the sensible one in this family, Miss Anne. Now that you're home, I hope you can stop your brother's foolishness. Imagine wanting to spend money on a merry-go-round! What was the man thinking of?"

"A carousel?" Anne stared at Mrs. Enke, not quite believing what she had heard. There had only been one carousel in Hidden Falls, and that had been the one her parents had rented as a birthday surprise for Anne and Jane. Though fifteen years had passed since then, Anne could still recall the magical sensation of climbing onto one of the painted ponies and whirling in circles as the music played. It had been the happiest birthday of her life.

Mrs. Enke's frown deepened. "That brother of yours turned the stable over to that carver man and his helpers. If that's not tomfoolery, I don't know what is."

Anne couldn't help smiling. A carousel. For the first time since the boat had docked in New York, she felt that this might be a real homecoming.

It was foolishness, the height of foolishness. Rob Ludlow picked up the gouge and positioned it over the wood. He was reputed to be a man of at least average intelligence. As such, he knew that he should not have gone to the station. He could have sent Mark or Luke or asked Brad Harrod to meet the train. But, no, even though afternoons were his most productive times, he hadn't listened to common sense. Instead, he'd stopped carving, walked over to Pleasant Hill, harnessed Susannah Deere's wagon and headed for the station, once he'd repaired the wobbly wheel. All told, it had taken an hour, an hour he could not afford.

And that wasn't the worst of it. Look at him now. He was standing here, a gouge in his hand, a perfect piece of wood in front of him. He ought to be pressing that gouge into the wood, turning the square block into a horse. That's what he ought to be doing, not staring into the distance, thinking of her.

She was different from the image he'd formed of her. Though he'd known she would no longer look exactly like the portrait Charles had shown him, he hadn't been prepared for the differences or the way they had made him feel. Anne and Jane Moreland were no longer identical twins. Logically, he'd known that. What he hadn't known was that Anne would be more beautiful than her sister. The last year had given her more than a new face; it had brought her a softness and a maturity that her sister still lacked. That softness had caused his breath to catch and his heart to pound. But what had surprised him the most was the hint of vulnerability that he'd seen in those beautiful blue eyes. It had made him want to gather her into his arms, to hold her close, and comfort her.

He couldn't, of course. Not today, not ever. What he had to do was carve the two remaining horses, create the menagerie and leave. He had already stayed in Hidden Falls far too long. What he sought wasn't here, and — tempting though it might be to stay long enough to banish the shadows from Anne Moreland's lovely eyes — that was one thing Rob couldn't do. Not if he was going to keep his promise.

Resolutely, Rob picked up the V-parting gouge and began to outline the horse. This was what he did best, create brightly colored ponies that made children — and sometimes adults — smile. *What he hadn't been able to do . . .* Rob frowned. There was no point in thinking of that. As soon as these animals were complete, he'd continue on the path he'd chosen. And this time he would succeed. He had to.

For a few minutes, Rob was able to forget everything but the pleasure that came as the shape of an animal emerged from the block of wood. Carvers called this "releasing" the animal, and for Rob, it was one of the most exciting parts of creating a carousel horse. There was something profoundly satisfying about being able to take a plain piece of wood and turn it into something that brought joy to others. He would think about that, not about what he hadn't accomplished and most definitely not about Anne Moreland's hauntingly beautiful eyes.

But when he heard the knock on the door and caught the faint scent of her perfume, Rob's thoughts scattered. She had come! Tossing a blanket over the lead horse, he sprinted to the Dutch door, thankful that, despite the heat, he'd kept both halves closed. Though the carousel itself would no longer be a surprise, at least the lead horse would be.

"May I come in, Mr. Ludlow?" She hadn't changed from her traveling clothes. Her skirt was wrinkled, the hem bore mud stains, and there was a piece of what appeared to be dust on her collar. It didn't matter. Anne Moreland was still the most beautiful woman he'd ever seen.

"I'd be honored," Rob said, thankful that

21

his voice did not betray just how much her appearance had affected him. "Only please call me 'Rob.' I'm not used to formality."

He saw the indecision on her face. She gazed at him for a long moment, those deep blue eyes so like her brother's reflecting her reluctance to disregard one of the precepts of polite society. Her mother, Rob suspected, had impressed on both of her daughters that only family or friends of long standing could be addressed by their first names. *His own mother . . .* Rob refused to complete the thought. Instead, he smiled at Anne, encouraging her to use his given name.

At length she nodded. "All right." She swallowed, then added, "Rob." The sense of accomplishment that he felt rush through him was out of all proportion to the single word she'd uttered.

Rob switched on several additional lights, dispelling the last of the shadows. More than anyone, Anne Moreland had a right to see this room. As she stepped into the stable that he'd turned into a carousel workshop, Anne looked around the large expanse, her eyes now sparkling with excitement. "So this is the woodworking you do." There was more than a hint of amusement in her voice.

Rob shrugged. He hadn't known whether

or not Charles had told Anne of the carousel, and so he'd deliberately underplayed his role. "How else would you describe it?"

She stretched out her hand and touched a painted mane, then ran her fingers over the jeweled eyes. Though she'd looked at each of the animals, she'd stopped at one of the simplest horses. Other than the lead horse, this was Rob's favorite. While some of the other steeds had fierce expressions, this one's head was tipped down, giving it a gentle appearance.

"Woodworking?" Anne raised an eyebrow. "I'm certain I can find a slightly more appropriate description." As she tipped her head to one side, considering, Rob saw pleasure reflected on her face. "If I were asked to explain what you're doing here, I'd say you were creating some of the most incredible objects I've ever seen." Her fingers continued their exploration, touching the horse's intricately carved saddle.

Rob's work had been praised by master carvers and carousel owners, but nothing those experts had said had pleased him the way Anne Moreland's words did. He swallowed deeply before he said, "If you like the horses, you can thank your brother. Charles gave me the freedom to create whatever I thought you'd like."

Her eyes widened, and this time there was no mistaking the surprise in them. "This is for me?" She looked around the room, clearly taken aback.

Rob nodded. "I wasn't sure how much Charles had told you about his plans for the carousel. He wanted it to welcome you home." Rob gestured toward the horse he'd only begun to carve and the sketches of the animals that hadn't been started. "As you can see, we're not quite finished."

Anne laid her hand on one of the horses' backs, as if to steady herself. She took a deep breath and looked at the workshop again. "My family will tell you that I'm rarely at a loss for words, but I don't know what to say."

Rob gazed at the woman whose blue eyes gleamed with pleasure, surprise, and what appeared to be humility. "You don't need to say anything at all. The pleasure on your face tells me that your brother didn't waste his money."

Anne shook her head. "Charles may have provided the money, but you're the one whose talent created these horses." Her smile was tremulous as she said, "Oh, Rob, they're breathtakingly beautiful."

"So are you."

CHAPTER TWO

He didn't mean it. Anne skewered the hat with her longest pin, then reached for her gloves. Of course he didn't mean it. She checked her reflection in the mirror, ensuring that her hat was on straight, frowning at the still unfamiliar face. Rob had been mouthing platitudes. No one — not even the doctor who had spent an almost incalculable amount of time and skill creating this face — would call her beautiful.

Anne was no longer beautiful. She knew that. Her beauty had been destroyed along with so much else that night. Still, she smiled as she walked down the front steps. The memory of Rob's words and the smile that had accompanied them warmed her more than the August sun. They might be platitudes, exaggerations, even lies, but that didn't keep her from wishing that they were true.

It was foolish, of course, to place such

importance on physical beauty when far more important things had been lost. Anne's smile faded and she bit the inside of her cheek, trying to quell the memories that returning home had revived. Placing one foot in front of the other, she walked briskly down the drive, turning left onto River Road. She couldn't undo the past. If there was anything she had learned in the last year, it was that. What mattered now was the future. What mattered was finding the perfect location and putting her plans into motion.

As she crossed the river, she fixed a smile onto her face. Knowing how quickly news traveled in Hidden Falls, it would be only a few minutes before curious townspeople just happened to be outside waiting to see what that high-priced doctor in Switzerland had been able to do to a face that had been scarred almost beyond recognition. The townspeople's curiosity was understandable and Anne wouldn't discourage it, particularly since she needed their help if her plan was to succeed.

That didn't mean, though, that she relished the thought of being stared at like an animal in a zoo. Or a carousel horse. Anne's lips curved into a genuine smile as she thought of the beautiful animals Rob Ludlow had carved. She'd focus on them and Charles's wonderful gift when the stares threatened her composure.

As she passed the train station and approached Mill Street, Anne grew pensive. If she could pick the ideal location for what she sought, it would be on Mill Street as close to the mill itself as possible. But, unless something had changed drastically while she was gone, there were no vacant buildings there. It was likely a waste of time to walk along Mill. Instead she'd continue one block further and would start on Main. Perhaps Charles had neglected to mention that one of the stores was empty. And even if there were no vacant buildings, the conversations with shopkeepers and customers might provide some leads.

Resolutely Anne continued into the middle of town. The corner of Main and Bridge housed four of Hidden Falls' institutions: the church with its wedding cake bell tower, the bank, a small hotel, and the tavern. None of those interested Anne today. Instead, she continued east toward the shops and the curiosity-driven townspeople.

"Good morning, Mrs. Morgan. It's nice to see you, Mrs. Schwartz." The vanguard had arrived in the form of two elderly women. Anne's smile was genuine as she greeted the ladies who had occasionally joined her mother for afternoon tea. It was reassuring to see that, while so many other things were altered, they hadn't changed. Mrs. Schwartz still had a stuffed bird perched on her hat, and her head bobbed a little when she spoke, almost as if she herself were a bird, drinking from a pool.

"Yes, I'm happy to be home again," Anne said in response to their questions. "I thought I'd see if the Mercantile had some of the new towels. Charles's letters were filled with descriptions of the designs Miss Deere had made for him." Her words were only half lies.

The two women nodded sagely. "We heard he went off to Paris, France to court her."

It was Anne's turn to nod. Talking about Charles and his possible marriage was safer than discussing her own plans for the future. That was something she had no intention of doing, not until she was ready to turn those plans into reality.

Her progress along Main Street was as slow as she'd anticipated, punctuated as it was by conversations with what felt like half the population of Hidden Falls. They were all polite, welcoming her back, and if their gaze lingered on her face longer than it would have a year ago, that was only to be expected. As was the fact that there were no empty stores on Main. She had walked all the way to Falls Street on the chance that one of the smaller boarding houses might have a vacant floor, but with the mill operating at full capacity, workers appeared to occupy every square inch. That was good for the town and only served to underscore the importance of finding a place where her dreams could take root.

Turning right on Falls, Anne made her way down the small hill. There was no question of what awaited her at the end of the street. The five-story red brick building had dominated the town from the day it was built, years before she was born. Her grandfather had founded Moreland Mills, capitalizing on the country's need for textiles as well as the energy that could be harnessed from the nearby waterfalls. Though his prospects were initially as rocky as the river bed, her grandfather had persevered, and the mill had transformed a small rural community into a town whose population produced some of the finest woven cotton products in the country. Moreland Mills became an institution.

Anne's father and now her brother continued the tradition of having a Moreland at the head of the town's most important industry. It was, Papa had told his children on numerous occasions, their responsibility to ensure that the workers could take pride in the goods that they produced and that they had a safe environment to both work and live. Contented workers, he said, produced better cloth than those who feared they'd lose a hand or worse. Anne nodded, remembering her father's admonitions. Though she would never be part of the mill operations, if all went as she had planned, Anne would soon be able to say that she was doing her share to create a contented workforce.

She walked slowly past the mill, her eyes drawn to the window that had once been her father's office and wondered if he would have approved of what she intended. Charles, she was certain, would object, at least initially. As for Jane, who knew what she would say? Ever since their ship had docked, she had been quieter than normal, seemingly caught up in thoughts that she didn't want to share. That was the change that disturbed Anne the most. For as long as she could remember, Jane had been not just her sister but also her best friend. And now . . .

"Anne!" The voice broke her reverie and

sent a wave of heat to Anne's face. She hadn't expected to see him here. "I thought you'd be resting from your journey." Rob lengthened his stride until he'd closed the distance between them. Doffing his hat in greeting, he smiled at her.

Anne returned the smile, hoping that he hadn't noticed the blush that stained her cheeks. This was the man who had called her beautiful, and that thought still had the power to embarrass her. Today would be different. Now that he was seeing her in the harsh light of mid-morning, he would realize how mistaken he had been. He wouldn't turn away. The little Anne knew of Rob Ludlow told her that he wouldn't be that cruel. But there would be something in his eyes that showed his feelings, and that something, she knew, would hurt as much as the doctor's knives had.

"I couldn't sleep," Anne said, pleased that her voice did not reflect the confusion that was displayed on her face. It was true that she had been unable to sleep. Rob didn't need to know that he was the reason she had tossed and turned, finally climbing from bed and staring at the moonless sky. He didn't need to know how deeply his words had touched her or that they had ignited a spark of hope that refused to be extinguished.

"I was anxious to see what changes the last year brought to Hidden Falls." That, too, was not a lie, though it wasn't the whole truth.

He was walking next to her, matching his pace to hers as easily as if they'd done this a hundred times. Fortunately this stretch of Mill had few pedestrians. The workers were inside the mill, and the town's other residents had little reason to traverse this block. Knowing how easily people could misconstrue a perfectly innocent walk, Anne was thankful that she and Rob were not observed. Though no one would openly question her, Rob would not escape the gossip so easily.

"Were there many changes?" It was a casual question, and yet something in the tone of his voice made Anne think that he cared about her response.

"Fewer than I expected," she admitted. Though she had changed, the town had not. "The biggest difference is the excitement over your carousel." To a person, everyone she had met had mentioned the merry-go-round. Some had told her that they thought Charles was foolish to spend money on something so frivolous, but the majority had reacted as she had, with eager anticipation.

Rob placed her hand on his arm. It was nothing more than a polite gesture, designed to steady her as they crossed the street. There was no reason that the touch of his hand should send another wave of color to her cheeks. For goodness sake, they were both wearing gloves. It wasn't as if anything unseemly were occurring.

"I keep telling you that it's your carousel." There was a hint of mirth in his voice. Surely he wasn't laughing at her confusion.

"And I keep telling you, Rob Ludlow, that you're the genius behind the carousel." To Anne's amazement, he appeared almost as uncomfortable with her praise as she had been with his use of the word "beautiful." "I can't blame the townspeople for their excitement," she continued. "All I could think about last night was those animals." And how Rob had called her beautiful.

"And all I could think about was seeing you riding one of them."

They had reached Bridge Street. The logical thing would be to turn left and return home. But when Rob looked down at her, a question in his eyes, Anne shook her head. "I haven't seen that part of Mill," she said, gesturing to the west. When she had left, the block had contained the school and a few houses in addition to the park. It was unlikely anything had changed, but extending the walk would give Anne more time with Rob, and that prospect was more appealing than she would admit to anyone.

"How long will it be before the carousel is finished?" she asked as they crossed Bridge.

A frown marred Rob's perfect face. "At least another month." Frustration tinged his voice. "It depends on how quickly Mark and Luke work." When Anne raised an eyebrow, he continued his explanation. "They're my assistants. They carve most of the bodies, leaving me to work on the heads."

That explained Mark and Luke's identity, but it didn't tell Anne why Rob was concerned about the delay in completing the carousel. Surely Charles wasn't hounding him. She wouldn't ask, though. Everyone was entitled to privacy.

"You're the first carousel carver I've met." And the most intriguing man she'd ever known. "What made you decide to carve horses?" They were passing the school now. Though empty because of the summer recess, Anne knew that within a few weeks, the building would be filled to capacity with children. By then this heat spell should have broken. Remembering how uncomfortable the school could be on a hot day, Anne hoped so — for her sake as well as the children's.

Unaware of the detour her thoughts had taken, Rob answered her question. "I've carved for almost as long as I can remember." There was a hint of sadness in Rob's voice, as if the memories weren't altogether pleasant. "When I was seven, I found an old knife and some wood in the barn and tried to turn it into a dog. You can imagine what happened." This time he smiled, and his blue eyes were warm with self-deprecating humor. "I cut my finger making something that didn't bear the slightest resemblance to a dog or, for that matter, anything living. But, even though the results were less than glorious, I was hooked."

Anne could picture the child Rob had been, rushing into the house to show his mother what he had created, the way she had the day she and Jane had twisted long grasses into what they claimed were dolls.

"Weren't your parents worried about your working with knives?" Even Charles, who had been the most intrepid of the Moreland children, wasn't allowed to play with anything as dangerous as a knife when he was seven. Their father had seen first hand the injuries that could result from careless use of equipment and was determined that his children, as well as his workers, would remain safe.

Rob turned his head to the side, almost as if he were trying to hide his expression. "I lived with an uncle after my parents died." Rob's voice was neutral, but the line of his jaw betrayed the emotion he refused to admit. "He thought carving was a foolish waste of time. The man was canny, though. Instead of forbidding me to carve, he simply gave me more chores so that I wouldn't have any free time."

"But you kept carving, anyway, didn't you?"

This time Rob's lips turned up in a grin. "I'm here, aren't I?"

Anne started to respond, to tell him how much she admired his perseverance, but as she turned her head to face him, her eyes were drawn to the house on the opposite side of the street. Unlike many of the private residences, it was built of brick. Anne liked that. Brick was less likely to burn than wood. The building appeared to be of average size. That was fine, too. She didn't need a large space. Anne guessed that there were two or three rooms on the first story and two small gabled rooms above. That was good. The youngest children could sleep upstairs, undisturbed by the sound of the others playing on the first floor.

The house itself had no distinguishing architectural style. That didn't matter. What had drawn Anne's attention was the fact that all the windows were boarded. Elation filled her heart and raced through her veins. This was it! This was what she had been seeking! The perfect size, the perfect building material, and it was vacant. She couldn't ask for more. Even the location was ideal. Although not next to the mill, the fact that it was close to the school was good. This was the perfect house in the perfect spot.

Though her mind whirled with the possibilities and she longed to learn who owned the house of her dreams, Anne struggled to keep her face from revealing her excitement. It was too soon to tell anyone. Besides, Rob was practically a stranger, even though they had progressed to a first name basis at a rate that would have appalled her mother.

Anne walked as sedately as she could to the corner, then turned around. Rob would think that she wanted to return home. She did. But more than that, she wanted to see the house — her house — again. And this time she would be on the correct side of the street and would have an even better view than she had before.

The day was uncomfortably warm without even a slight breeze to dissipate the heat.

The birds that would normally be chirping were silent, perhaps conserving their energy. Smoke from the mill hung in the heavy air, turning it pale gray. It was the kind of day Anne had always dreaded, but today that didn't matter. All that mattered was that she had taken a giant step toward making her dream real.

"It may be presumptuous of me to say so," Rob said as they walked back toward the center of town, "but you don't appear to be a woman who's taking a casual stroll."

Anne felt the blood drain from her face. *How had he guessed?* Surely she hadn't been obvious in the glances she had darted at the house. Surely, even though her hand still rested on his arm, he hadn't felt her pulse race when she'd seen it.

"But that's precisely what I'm doing," she insisted. She wouldn't meet Rob's gaze, lest he see the lie reflected in her eyes.

He slowed his pace. *Was it chance that they were in front of her house?* "Is it?" he asked. Almost against her will, Anne looked up at him. Those blue eyes that somehow seemed familiar were serious. "Again, perhaps I'm being presumptuous, but you strike me as a woman with a mission."

He had guessed. Somehow, something she had done had given him the clues. Anne took a deep breath and exhaled slowly, trying to formulate her response. She could deny it. She ought to deny it. After all, she hadn't told anyone — not even Jane — of her plans. Surely her family ought to learn what she intended before anyone else. But Charles was in Paris and Jane was rarely home. Still, she shouldn't confide in Rob. Though she knew that, Anne could not deny how much she wanted to share her ideas and her excitement with someone. No, not with just anyone. She wanted to tell Rob Ludlow. An hour ago she might not have dared, but now that she knew Rob had dealt with disapproving relatives and had succeeded despite them, Anne was certain he would understand what she wanted to do.

"I'm looking for a building to buy or rent." Now that the words were spoken, there was no going back.

Anne no longer made any pretense of strolling. They stood in front of the red brick house, but for the moment her attention was focused on Rob. *How would he react?* Without any apparent hesitation, he nodded, as if there were nothing unusual about a single woman planning to buy a building. "What will you do with it?" There was no censure in his voice. All Anne heard was interest.

She took another deep breath, then exhaled slowly. "I want to provide a place for the workers' smallest children to stay while their parents are at the mill."

"So that both parents can work." Rob completed the sentence.

Anne shook her head. It wasn't that simple. "Most of the time both parents do work. Until they're old enough for school, the children are left with either older children or elderly neighbors. The problem is, neither one is able to care for them properly."

"I see." They were two short words, but the way Rob pronounced them made Anne's heart sing, for it was clear that not only did he not disapprove, but he thought the idea was a good one. Her instincts had been accurate; he did understand.

"This is the house I'm considering." Anne gestured toward the brick building with the boarded-up windows that she already thought of as her house.

"A good location." Again, there was approval in Rob's voice, and again Anne felt her spirits rise. She'd been determined to do this, with or without anyone's approbation, but there was no denying how good it felt to have Rob both understand and approve.

As they resumed their walk, he asked whether Charles was aware of her plans.

"Not yet," Anne admitted. "And," she answered Rob's unspoken question, "he probably won't like the idea. Charles has always been protective of Jane and me, and that tendency has only increased in the last year."

They turned onto Bridge and walked past the park. Anne smiled as she watched four youngsters engage in a game of tag. How often had she and Jane tried to enlist Charles and Brad Harrod in their games, only to be told that the big boys had no time for silly games? So much had changed since then.

Rob laid his hand on top of Anne's as they crossed the street. "You're going to open the nursery, with or without Charles's approval." It was a statement, not a question.

"Yes, I am." That was one of the promises Anne had made to herself, that nothing would dissuade her. Though he hadn't asked, Anne wanted to tell Rob why she had made the decision that might alienate her from her family. "You know that Jane and I were in Switzerland for a year." Everyone in Hidden Falls knew that and the reason why. "While we were there, I saw how the nurses and staff worried about their children and

41

who was caring for them. I don't mean to imply that they neglected me or their other patients. They didn't. It was simply that I realized they couldn't devote all their attention to their work if they were worried about their children. Seeing them made me think about what it must be like for the workers at Moreland Mills." Anne's footsteps slowed as she and Rob climbed the hill. "I hate to admit this, but until that day, I never really thought about the mill hands. It sounds so selfish, but I took them for granted and never realized what their lives must be like. Now I want to help them."

They reached the crest, and Rob stopped to let Anne catch her breath. Though his eyes were serious, Anne saw approval radiating from them. "I can't predict your brother's reaction, but — speaking for myself — I think it's a good idea." He looked down the hill at the mill. "You talked about the parents, but your nursery will be good for the children, too." Rob paused, then added, "Children deserve to be happy."

Though he said nothing more, Rob's eyes darkened with an emotion that Anne could not identify but one that made her heart reach out to him. She tightened her grip on his arm, wanting to comfort him, then pulled her hand away. It was foolish to think that she could help him. He was a grown man, a man who had overcome obstacles to make a success of his life. He didn't need her. Of course he didn't.

She had a sense of déjà vu as she guided the horse toward the train station. How many times had she driven this same route to meet Charles's train? She had lost count over the years. All Anne knew was that it had become a tradition, and the sole time she hadn't met him at the depot had been the day . . . Anne clenched her teeth. She wouldn't think about that day. She wouldn't wonder why Charles had taken an earlier train or what had caused him to leave their home so precipitously. And she most definitely would not think of what had happened that night. What mattered was today and the future she would create.

Today was already different. In the past, she'd driven one of the Moreland horses. Today she'd climbed the small hill to Susannah Deere's house and had borrowed one of her horses and wagons. How strange it had felt to see Megan and Moira O'Toole working at Pleasant Hill instead of Fairlawn and to realize that the only horses in the once famous Moreland stable were Rob's painted ponies. So much had changed.

Anne tied the horse and walked to the platform where she and Jane had disembarked less than a week ago. The train whistled as it crossed the street, then screeched to a halt in front of the depot just as it did every day at this time. The doors to the passenger car opened, just as they did every day. But then a beautiful brunette stepped out, a small white dog cradled in her arms. That, Anne knew, did not happen every day. Nor were beautiful women normally followed by tall blond men, their faces partially obscured by black dogs that appeared to be licking their noses. Though she'd never seen the woman before, there was no doubting the man's identity.

"Charles!" All sense of decorum fled as Anne launched herself into her brother's arms. "Oh, I'm so glad you're home!" The black dog yipped, then swiveled its head to stare at the stranger. As its tongue reached out, Anne took a step backward. No matter how good it was to see Charle, there was another passenger to greet. Charles's telegram had announced that he and his bride would be arriving on this train. The man who had once made a pact that he would not marry before his thirtieth birthday had changed his mind, and this woman was the reason.

"You must be Susannah," Anne said, extending her hand to the beautiful brunette. "Welcome to the family." She looked from the woman who was now her sister-in-law to her brother, noting the changes on that dearly beloved face. "Charles told me you were a painter, but he neglected to mention that you were also a miracle worker."

The woman's dark brown eyes sparkled with mirth as she gave Charles a smile so filled with love that it made Anne's heart ache. "A miracle worker? He's called me many things, but that's not one of them." As the white dog squirmed, Susannah placed him on the ground. Seconds later he was joined by the black dog, and the two raced from one end of the platform to the other.

Anne smiled, both at the dogs' antics and the changes she'd observed in her brother. "All I can say is that I've never seen my brother looking so happy. It must be a miracle." The lines of strain that had marked Charles's face were gone, replaced with a smile that told Anne more clearly than words how deeply he loved his wife. This change was a good one.

Charles shrugged as he directed the porter toward his and Susannah's trunks. "This woman never changes," he said with a rueful smile at Anne. "Even as a child, she liked to tease me. I had hoped that she would change with maturity, but — alas — she has not."

He was wrong, of course. Anne had changed, and so had he. The difference was, Charles's changes were by choice whereas hers were the result of circumstances. "It's fortunate I brought the large wagon," Anne said, trying not to think of the changes Charles was too polite to acknowledge. "It appears that you brought half of France home with you." The pile of trunks was growing to an alarming height.

"I'm afraid that most of them are mine," Susannah said. "Your brother convinced me that every woman needs a French trousseau. And then there are all my painting supplies."

"I'd say that it's fortunate Mrs. Enke insisted on preparing the largest guest room for you." She had declared Charles's old room unsuitable for a couple, and the south wing where Anne's parents had resided was no longer habitable.

"I'm sorry, Anne." Charles led his wife toward the wagon that three porters were filling with trunks. "I should have told you that we're going to live in Susannah's house."

Another change, and one Anne hadn't expected. Still, she couldn't blame her brother. Not only would the newlyweds have more privacy at Pleasant Hill, but they'd also be escaping the unhappy memories that clung to Fairlawn.

"I understand." And she did. "But I hope you'll have dinner with us. Mrs. Enke is cooking a roast with new potatoes, and I heard a rumor that there would be lemon meringue pie."

Susannah's brown eyes sparkled as she gave her husband a fond glance. "You see, Charles, your housekeeper has a soft spot for you, after all." Susannah patted the white dog's head, then lifted him into the back of the wagon. "Your brother went to every pastry shop in Paris, looking for lemon tarts, but he said none of them compared to Mrs. Enke's pies."

Charles wrinkled his nose. "If you're going to continue telling tales, Susannah dear, I'll tell Anne about your search for white paint."

The blush that stained Susannah's face made Anne realize that there was more to the story than simply shopping.

"Perhaps we should get these dogs home,"

Susannah said, picking up the black one.

"Mrs. Enke told me she had saved bones for them."

As Charles reached for the reins, he laughed. "Now that is a true miracle."

But the miracle was seeing Charles so happy and hearing his laughter. The year had wrought changes in both of them. Charles's changes were good ones, whereas hers . . . Anne forced a smile. She wouldn't think about things that could not be altered.

It was the smoke that awakened her. Tendrils drifted beneath the door, rising in delicate wisps. For a second, she stared at them, mesmerized by their beauty. Never before had she seen fingers of smoke in her room. Never before had their dark hue threatened to obscure the moonlight. Her head clouded by sleep and the smoke, she smiled. Then reality intruded.

Smoke! It was wrong, wrong, wrong! Anne tossed off the blankets and raced across the room, scarcely aware of the strangely warm floor beneath her bare feet. As she opened the door, she was faced with a wall of gray, the smoke so dense that it appeared impenetrable. She looked in both directions. No! Dear God, no! The smoke was coming from the wing her parents shared. She had to reach them.

"Jane! Help me, Jane!" Anne flung open the door to her sister's room. There was less smoke here, and the moonlight was bright enough that Anne could see the empty chamber. Jane was not here. Her carefully made bed said she had not retired for the evening. She was probably sitting in the gazebo, the way she did so many nights when she couldn't sleep. Jane was safe; their parents were not.

Heedless of the danger, Anne ran back into the hallway, trying desperately not to breathe in the lethal fumes. She had to find her parents. She had to be sure they were safe. But nothing could stop her fears from mounting as the ever thickening smoke brought tears to her eyes. If Mama and Papa were awake, they would have come to her room. They would have taken her and Jane from the house.

Her heart thudding with dread, Anne pushed open the door to her parents' room. The smoke was thicker here, so thick that she could see nothing, not even the light from the door to the verandah. Anne gasped in horror. As tears streamed down her face, she heard the crackle of the flames and the horrible sound of fire consuming wood.

"Mama! Papa! Wake up!" She screamed the

words again and again, forcing herself to ignore the burning in the back of her throat. But there was no response, only the sickening sound of the flames feeding on wood.

They were here! Anne knew it, just as she knew that she had to get them out of the room, out of the house. Closing her eyes until they were only slits, she moved from memory, approaching the bed where she knew they must be. Yes! That was Mama's arm. Anne tugged, then slid her arms around her mother. Something hurt. She wouldn't think about that. What mattered was getting Mama onto the verandah. Another foot, and they'd be there. Fumbling in the darkness, Anne found the handle. With a wrench she pulled the door open, and though it took a Herculean effort, she lifted her mother and dragged her outside.

Papa was so heavy! "Wake up, Papa!" If only he could walk. If only he could help her get him to safety. But he said nothing. Anne tightened her grip on him and tugged. She couldn't carry him. Her arms were too weak, and there was something wrong with them, something that made them hurt, just as her face and throat hurt. She couldn't think about that, not now, not when Papa was still inside. Anne tugged again, pulling him out of the bed and onto the floor. Then slowly, inch by inch, she dragged her father across the floor and over the threshold.

When the fire brigade arrived, they found her on the verandah, one arm wrapped around each parent, her face and arms so badly burned that a fireman wept from pity.

Anne awoke, her body wracked with shudders. It was always the same. No matter how many months passed, the nightmare was always the same, destroying all hopes of sleep by forcing her to relive the worst night of her life. And no matter how often she relived it, no matter how valiantly she battled the fire, she couldn't change the ending. She had failed.

This time would be different. Rob dipped his pen into the inkwell and signed the letter. This time he would succeed. He sealed the envelope, then reached for another piece of paper. He wouldn't count the number of letters he'd written, the number of towns he'd visited, or the number of people he'd questioned. He most certainly would not count the number of dead ends he'd reached.

This time would be different. This time the doctor or the minister or the mayor would respond that yes, Edith Ludlow — or perhaps she was calling herself Edith Bar-

ton — lived in their town.
This time he would not fail.

CHAPTER THREE

"You've made a lot of progress on your plans." Rob walked around the table, looking at Anne's penciled drawing from all angles. His brow furrowed, the crease between his eyes mirroring the cleft in his chin, Rob was the picture of a pensive man. Anne clasped her hands together to hide her nervousness as she waited for his reaction.

It was late morning, a time she knew that Rob was usually alone in the workshop. Though she enjoyed Mark and Luke's bantering and their occasional attempts to convince her she should help them carve one of the remaining animals' bodies, this was one time when Anne wanted no audience. Rob was the only one who knew of her dreams, and he was the only one she wanted to see the plans she'd worked on so carefully.

"Looks good." He nodded his approval,

then punctuated it with a grin as he walked back to her side of the table. "I like it."

Anne matched Rob's grin, though she wasn't certain whether she was smiling from pleasure or relief or a combination of the two. She had told herself that nothing would stop her from opening the nursery, but it was good — no, it was more than good; it was wonderful — that Rob viewed her plans favorably. Though the day was heavily overcast, Anne felt as if the sun had just broken through the clouds.

"I couldn't have gotten this far without you," she told him. It was true. One of the maddening things about living in Hidden Falls was knowing that no one in the town would consider selling a house to her, or to any woman, for that matter. Men handled affairs of a financial nature, or so the townspeople believed. Anne wondered what the good citizens of Hidden Falls would think if they knew how many hours her father had spent explaining the mill's balance sheets to her or how often he'd asked her opinion of suppliers' proposals.

But they didn't know, and if she'd started asking questions about the house — her house — within ten minutes, some helpful soul would have told Charles. He would have to know eventually, but only when

Anne was ready to make the actual purchase. She wasn't prepared yet, which was why she hadn't asked Philip Biddle or Ralph Chambers, the men who'd been her father's advisors, for their assistance. Like the rest of the town, the former banker and attorney would have thought it their duty to consult Charles. And Big Brother, Anne was certain, would have disapproved. He might be blissfully happy as a newlywed and more relaxed now that the accidents at the mill had ceased, but Anne doubted he would support her plan to become a businesswoman.

And so it had been Rob who'd made the inquiries. In one morning, he had accomplished everything she'd needed. He'd learned that the owners of the house, the Brickers, were willing to rent it but would prefer to sell the building. He'd obtained the asking price, and then, claiming that he was considering moving to Hidden Falls permanently, Rob had gone inside the house. Once indoors, he'd assessed its structural strength and measured each of the rooms. Returning to the carousel workshop, Rob had sketched the floor plan for Anne. Then, when another man might have made suggestions, he'd simply handed the plans to her, as if he understood that this was her venture and that she needed to make the decisions.

"You know I'm glad to help you," Rob said, his forefinger tracing the outline of the partition she wanted to put in one of the second floor bedrooms so that the youngest children's sleep area would be separated from the toddlers'. "What you're planning to do is important."

Anne nodded. "I think so. I only wish there were something I could do to repay you for all the time you spent helping me with this." She gestured toward the plans. Though Rob had not seen the finished plans until today, Anne had discussed alternative arrangements with him and had found his advice invaluable.

"I never expected anything in return." The tone of Rob's voice made Anne think he was insulted by her words, but his voice was once more even as he asked, "Have you thought about who's going to do the painting?" Surely she had been mistaken in thinking he was annoyed.

"Promise you won't laugh," Anne said, trying to keep their conversation light. She certainly did not want to insult Rob again, not when he'd been so kind to her. Anne paused for effect, then pointed a finger at herself. "I thought I'd do it." The entire building, Rob had told her, needed at least one coat of whitewash.

A raised eyebrow greeted her answer. "Have you ever painted a room?"

"No, but I never ran a nursery, either. How hard can it be?"

This time Rob chuckled. "It's not difficult, but it is a lot of work. You'll be amazed how large those rooms seem when you start wielding a paintbrush."

"I'm not afraid of hard work."

"I didn't say you were." He studied the plans again, as if he were calculating the square footage of each room.

"I know," Anne conceded. Unlike Charles, Rob had never been either judgmental or protective. He had always acted as if she were a capable adult. She glanced out the window, her spirits suddenly as dismal as the day. Taking a deep breath, she turned to face Rob again. "It's not your fault. It's simply that ever since the fire, everyone wants to treat me as if I'm made of glass and will shatter from the slightest strain." Rob's head jerked up, and she forced her eyes to meet his. "I was burned, Rob. Badly burned. And despite everything the doctor in Switzerland did, my face will never look like Jane's and my arms will always bear scars. Those are the facts. I can't change them, but that doesn't stop me from being

57

able to paint a room or care for children."

Rob was silent for a moment, his eyes more serious than she'd ever seen them. As he gazed at her, something tugged at Anne's memory. Where had she seen eyes like that? At length Rob spoke. "Do you feel better now?"

Strangely enough, she did. Anne nodded. "I'm sorry you had to listen to that." What had come over her, baring her heart to him that way? She had told no one, not even Jane, how much she hated being treated like spun glass, but here she was, confiding her innermost thoughts to a man she'd known for less than a month. Mama would have been appalled.

As if he sensed her embarrassment, Rob said, "The first man who taught me to carve horses told me that people are like volcanoes. Sometimes they need to vent some steam or they'll erupt."

Though Anne had never seen a volcano, she had read enough about them to realize that venting might prevent some natural disasters. "He was a wise man." She started to roll up the plans, then stopped. If the man had told Rob about volcanoes, Rob himself must have been venting. Though she knew she shouldn't pry, she couldn't stop herself from asking, "When you vent steam, what's the reason?"

Once again, silence greeted her words. Rob looked out the small window, and Anne sensed he was trying to decide how much to tell her. "I guess if I had to pick one thing, it would be the worries of being an independent carver." Rob gestured toward the giraffe whose head he'd been carving when Anne had entered the workshop. "I worked for other companies in the past. Loof, Dentzel, the Philadelphia Toboggan Company." He listed three of the most famous creators of merry-go-rounds. "It was good secure work, and I learned a lot from them. Eventually, though, I wanted to develop my own style, not mimic theirs. I wanted to carve more than horses." He pointed toward the giraffe. That, with the elephant, the bear and the ostrich, would turn the ordinary carousel into what carvers called a menagerie. "I'd never created one of those exotic animals, but your brother took a chance on me, and I'm grateful for that."

Anne had wondered about the special animals just as she wondered why Charles had demolished their grandmother's gazebo to place the carousel there, but she hadn't had the opportunity to ask her brother either question. Rob had answered one of her unspoken questions, though not the one she had posed to him. "Then what is it that worries you?"

"The responsibility. Money, to put it bluntly." Rob walked toward the other partially carved animals. "Mark and Luke depend on me. They left Dentzel to join me." Lines formed between his eyes. "What happens to them if there's no one other than Charles who wants me to build a carousel? I'm not sure Dentzel or PTC would take them back."

"There will be other carousels to build," Anne said. "I know there will be." Just as she knew that concerns about Mark and Luke's welfare were only part of what troubled Rob. There had been something in his expression when he'd started to answer her that had made her think carousel worries were minor compared to something else. It was equally obvious that he had no intention of revealing that something else. Either he wasn't ready to vent, or he didn't want her to see the smoke and steam. "Charles will . . ."

"What will I do?"

Startled, Anne turned toward the doorway. Her brother stood there, casually leaning against the frame. *How long had he been there? How much had he heard?*

"Is it dinner time already?" she asked, hoping to distract him. Occasionally Charles would stop at Fairlawn on his way from the mill to the noon meal at Pleasant Hill. It still seemed strange to realize that what Anne thought of as Susannah's house was now her brother's home.

"Almost." Anne's hopes of a reprieve plummeted as Charles stepped into the room. His gaze moved from Anne to Rob, then lit on the table. Though Rob stood in front of it, he couldn't block the view. If only she had rerolled the plans, but she hadn't. "What's this?" Charles demanded, striding toward the table.

Anne took a deep breath. Though she wasn't ready to tell Charles about her dream and how she was going to make it come true, now she had no choice. No one would ever mistake her floor plans for the drawings of carousel animals that normally covered the table.

"They're plans for the nursery I'm going to open." She laid a protective hand on one corner, marveling that her voice did not reflect her nervousness. Charles couldn't stop her, she reminded herself, but he could make her life difficult. "It's the Bricker house, across from the school."

Though she kept her hand on the plans,

Anne looked up at her brother. Those blue eyes so like her own widened in surprise. "A nursery? What kind of nonsensical idea is that?" Charles took a step closer, frowning as he saw the sketch of cribs and tables.

"It's not nonsense, Charles." Anne straightened her shoulders and met her brother's stare. She would not let him cow her. "I want to do something useful with my life. I can't spend my days planning menus, making needlepoint cushions or working in the garden." Their mother had found that fulfilling, but she had also had three children to raise. Raising children, Anne knew, was not part of her future, though caring for other people's children would be.

"And just who do you think will come to this nursery?" Though it was obvious that Charles was trying to control his anger, his voice rose. In response, Rob took a step closer to Anne. Her eyes met his for a second, and she nodded, acknowledging the silent support he was providing.

"The nursery is for the mill workers' children," she said, deliberately lowering her voice. That was the technique her mother had used to quell arguments.

"That riff raff?" Charles pounded one fist into his other hand, his fury evident. "Anne,

62

you can't be serious. Why, you could catch some horrible disease from them."

Anne nodded slowly. That was another method her mother had used to great effect when one of the children was arguing with her. She would appear to agree, then politely explain why they were wrong. Though she nodded, Anne wasn't certain she could manage the polite rebuttal. "I see." She took a deep breath. "These people that you call the riff raff are good enough to work in the mill and put food on our table but not good enough for anyone to care about them once they step outside the hallowed walls of Moreland Mills." Anne lowered her voice again. "They're a necessary evil to you, aren't they, Charles? I imagine you'd gladly replace them with machines if you could."

The barb hit his mark, for Charles's face reddened. He was silent for a second, then his upper lip curled in obvious disdain. "This is Matt Wagner's idea, isn't it?"

Matt had been Charles's childhood nemesis, and it appeared that the enmity between them hadn't lessened with the passage of time. Anne had heard that Matt had returned to Hidden Falls earlier this year, planning to use his Harvard Law degree to better the workers' lot in life. That would have put Matt and Charles back where they'd always been, butting heads like two wild animals. That was bad enough, but today was worse. This morning it was she and Charles who were adversaries. In the past, Charles had always won their arguments, taking advantage of his greater age and size. Today would be different.

"Do you know how insulting your suggestion is?" Anne demanded. "You're insinuating that I couldn't form an idea of my own. That's where you're wrong, Charles. The nursery is my idea — my dream — and I've been thinking about it for almost a year now. As for Matt, I haven't seen him since Jane and I returned."

Though he appeared slightly mollified by the fact that Matt had not been the instigator, Charles's face was still flushed with anger. "You call it a dream. I'd call it a nightmare."

As Rob took a step forward, Anne shook her head. This was her battle. While it was comforting to have a knight in shining armor standing at her side, she would fight her brother alone.

"Opening a nursery is not a nightmare, Charles. It's something Hidden Falls needs, and it's something I'm going to do."

He shook his head, and the way he clenched and unclenched his fists told Anne just how angry he was. Other than his periodic scuffles with Matt, Anne had not seen this side of her brother. "No, you will not open a nursery or do anything else that puts you in contact with the mill workers. I'm the head of this family, and it's my responsibility to stop you from making a serious mistake." Charles paused, then narrowed his eyes slightly as he continued. "How do you think you'll be able to buy that house if I don't agree?"

That was the crux of the problem. Even though Anne had enough money to buy the house, the Brickers would not sell it to her, a woman. She had thought she would be able to persuade Charles to handle the transaction on her behalf, but evidently that was not going to happen.

"I'll lease it for you, Anne." Rob spoke softly but firmly.

She turned toward him, startled by the offer. Rob had no way of knowing that she had money in her own name, yet now, only a few minutes since he had told her that he was worried about money, he was offering her financial support that he could ill afford. "You'd do that for me?" she asked, more warmed by his words than she'd have thought possible. Few men other than Matt Wagner dared to defy Charles, yet here was

Rob, whose livelihood depended on Charles, risking his own security and that of his assistants to help her. Though possibly foolhardy, it was an incredibly generous gesture.

"I'd do it for you and for those children," Rob said. He took a step toward Charles, his demeanor changing from conciliatory to confrontational. "I know you hired me to build a carousel, not interfere in your family's affairs, but I can't help it. Anne's idea is a good one."

"The whole idea is preposterous."

Anne shook her head. Charles would never agree to her plan; that was obvious. He would probably actively oppose her. Somehow she would deal with that, but Charles ought to understand the benefits the nursery could bring. "Your workers will be more productive if they're not worried about their children," she told him.

"Save your arguments." Charles unclenched his fists and looked from Anne to Rob and back again, a speculative expression on his face. "Nothing you can say will make me like the idea, but . . ."

"But?" It was the first time she had heard the slightest hesitation in his voice.

Charles shrugged his shoulders. "I know when I'm outnumbered. I'll buy the house for you."

For a second Anne was too surprised to react. It wasn't like Charles to capitulate. But he had, and she'd won. Flinging her arms around him, Anne hugged her brother. "Oh, Charles! Thank you!"

He shrugged again. This was the Charles she knew, pretending that his generosity was of no account. "It seems to be my fate to be surrounded by strong-willed women who won't rest until I agree to their whims."

The nursery wasn't a whim, but Anne wasn't going to argue with him, not when he'd consented to helping her turn her dream into reality. She flashed a smile at Rob, who was looking ill at ease. As an only child, he would never have experienced sibling squabbles. To an outsider, they probably appeared more serious than they were.

Turning back to Charles, Anne raised an eyebrow. "You said women, as in plural. Who's the other one?" She doubted Jane had had any confrontations with their brother, at least not since they'd returned from Europe. Though Jane's shyness had faded, she'd never been one to argue. Instead, she would quietly do whatever she wanted. Forgiveness, she had once told Anne, was sometimes easier to obtain than permission.

The expression on Charles's face said the

answer should be apparent. "My wife, of course. When I asked Rob to build the carousel for you, I planned to keep it here at Fairlawn." Anne nodded. That explained the demolition of the gazebo. "It was Susannah who insisted that we move it to the park. She said you'd want everyone in Hidden Falls to enjoy it."

"Your wife is a wise woman." Anne couldn't imagine not sharing Rob's magnificent animals with the whole town.

Charles pulled out his watch as casually as if there had been no altercation. "My wise wife will be angry if I keep dinner waiting." Nodding at Rob, Charles left the workshop, almost sprinting in his eagerness to see Susannah again.

Anne tried not to sigh at the thought that the fire had destroyed her chance of having a man look at her the way Charles looked at Susannah, of finding a man who was willing to look at scars every day of his life. She wouldn't think about that. Instead, she'd focus on the nursery and the victory she'd just won. A victory that she owed to the man standing next to her.

Anne laid her hand on Rob's arm. "I don't know how to thank you," she said. "If it weren't for you, Charles would never have agreed." The turning point had been the moment when Rob had volunteered to lease the house. Charles hadn't wanted to be outdone by a man he'd hired.

As Rob covered her hand with his, Anne felt the calluses that came from honest labor. "You were pretty persuasive yourself."

"Persuasive?" Anne couldn't help laughing. "Charles would say I was stubborn."

"Then it must run in the family."

Her heart lighter than it had been since she'd returned to Hidden Falls, Anne smiled at the man who'd helped make her dream come true.

Rob picked up the spoon gouge. This was the tool he used for deep cuts like the sculpting of an animal's nostrils. He, Mark, and Luke were working on the second row of animals that Charles had commissioned. Though they were smaller and less elaborate than the outside row, Rob had insisted that they be no less beautiful. This detailed carving was painstaking, but he enjoyed it, as he did every step that transformed a block of wood into a carousel animal.

Working didn't stop his thoughts from whirling, remembering the scene that had taken place here just a few hours ago. Anne had reminded him of one of those Greek warrior goddesses, her eyes flashing with determination as she faced her brother's anger. The woman was beautiful, more beautiful than her sister, and yet she seemed unaware of it. Did she believe that a man couldn't see beneath the faint scars to the radiance that came from within?

As for Charles, it was obvious the man didn't realize how fortunate he was. It wasn't simply that he owned the mill and had a beautiful wife who adored him. Those ought to be enough to make any man happy, but Charles had more. Rob took a step back and squinted, picturing the giraffe's face when he'd added the jeweled eyes and painted the features. A giraffe was a gentle animal. It must be his imagination that the horse reminded him of Charles at his most imperious.

That man's cup truly overfloweth. In addition to the mill, his wife, and those two mischievous dogs that appeared to rule the roost, Charles was part of a family. A real family. The man had been blessed with two sisters. Oh, he might call them stubborn and he might argue with them, but nothing could take them away from him.

Rob gripped the gouge so tightly that his knuckles whitened. He'd give anything, anything on earth, to still have a sister!

"A nursery? What other secrets have you been hiding from me?" Jane fisted her hands on her hips and glared at Anne with an expression so similar to Charles's that Anne had to fight to control her smile.

"None," she said. *Other than the fact that I have a new friend and I'm worried about him.* But, though she shared many things with her twin, that was one secret Jane didn't need to know. She had come back from her morning ride earlier than usual today and had found Anne in the room that had been their mother's office, looking through her recipes.

"When are you planning to open it?" Jane sank into the chair on the other side of the desk. Strands of hair had escaped from both her side and back combs, giving normally neat Jane a slightly disheveled appearance. That and the glow on her cheeks were undoubtedly the result of her ride.

"I'll open it as soon as I can get the rooms painted and furnished." Closing the book of receipts, Anne leaned forward. "I thought I might take some of the toys from the attic and maybe the cribs you and I used. Would you mind?"

Jane shrugged. "It doesn't seem as if you and I'll be needing them any time soon."

Anne knew she wouldn't, but she wasn't so certain about her sister. "If you marry Brad . . ."

A year ago before the fire that had changed all of their lives, Anne had thought that her sister and Brad Harrod were on the verge of announcing their engagement. It was a move that would have pleased both sets of parents, for the Harrods were the Morelands' closest friends as well as their nearest neighbors. Anne knew that there had been speculation that the engagement would be made official the night of the Harrods' party. But then something — Anne still didn't know what — had made Charles storm out of Fairlawn, declaring he'd never again set foot in his parents' house, and in the aftermath of that argument, no one had been in the mood for a party. They'd stayed home, and then the fire had started. Would it have been different if they'd gone to the Harrods'? Would their parents still be alive? Anne didn't know. What she did know was that speculation was useless.

Jane's thoughts did not take the detour Anne's had. She leapt to her feet and glared at her sister. "I am not going to marry Brad," she declared. "Not this year, not ever. Charles has Susannah. You have the nursery. I want my own life, and that life does not include Brad Harrod."

Anne tried not to stare, though her sister's vehemence surprised her. "I'm sorry I mentioned it," she said. Now would not be a good time to tell Jane that Mrs. Harrod was planning a party in their honor. Instead, deliberately changing the subject, Anne asked, "Are you going into town this afternoon?"

"Probably. Why?"

She gestured toward the envelopes she'd placed on the corner of the desk. "Would you mind taking these to the post office?" They were orders for children's books for the nursery.

Rifling through the stack of letters, Jane's lips curved into a smile. "It appears that you're in competition with Rob."

"What do you mean?"

Jane shrugged. "I heard he writes more letters than anyone in Hidden Falls."

Anne couldn't help wondering why.

Chapter Four

Anne picked up the last of the quilts that she'd earmarked for the nursery, then folded it carefully in quarters. She was one step closer to having everything ready. Soon. Her heart sang with anticipation. Soon the children of Hidden Falls would have a clean, safe, friendly place to spend the day.

Anne straightened and rubbed the small of her back, easing the cramp that too much bending had caused. It was almost miraculous how smoothly everything had gone since Charles had agreed to buy the Bricker house. Even this task had proven pleasant. When she had started rummaging through the trunks in the attic, searching for things to take to the nursery, Anne had been afraid that opening the trunk with the quilts would be like lifting the lid on Pandora's Box, that memories would fly out, overwhelming her with sadness. That hadn't happened. It was true that the quilts had evoked memories, but to Anne's surprise, they had been happy ones. She could picture her mother carefully piecing the large blue quilt, and the green one reminded her of the summer Mama had taught Anne and Jane to quilt. They'd each made a coverlet for their dolls. Though the stitches had been crooked and the pieces misaligned, Mama had declared each one a masterpiece and had insisted that the girls show their handiwork to their father.

When she had chosen a few quilts to cover the beds at the nursery, Anne could picture her mother smiling as if she approved of Anne's plans. That felt good, as did the knowledge that while Charles might never approve of the nursery, he was no longer actively opposing it.

The nursery was almost finished. Anne chuckled when she thought of how right Rob had been when he'd told her that painting would be hard work. It was, and Anne's arms had ached for days afterwards. But what she remembered most about that day was not the effort involved but the fact that Rob and Jane had helped her paint. Susannah had brought them a picnic lunch, then stayed to wield a brush. Throughout the day they had told stories and laughed as they'd turned the dingy walls white, and when Anne had managed to get a smudge of paint on her nose, Susannah had announced that she wanted to paint her portrait, white nose and all.

Anne smiled, thinking of her brother's bride. Though she had been prepared to welcome Susannah to the family, she hadn't expected the instant feeling of kinship that she'd felt for her. In just a few days, Susannah seemed like another sister, not a sister-in-law. And with Jane absent from Fairlawn for most of the day, Susannah filled a void in Anne's life. When Anne needed a break, she knew that Susannah was waiting at Pleasant Hill to provide tea, scones, and something far more important: companionship.

The sound of footsteps on the pine floor surprised Anne. It was too early for Jane to be home, and no one else came into the attic.

"You have a visitor, Miss Anne," Mrs. Enke announced, her words coming in short bursts as she tried to catch her breath after climbing the attic stairs.

Anne raised an eyebrow, both at the thought of her unexpected guest and the housekeeper's flushed face. "A visitor?"

The older woman pressed her hand to her chest, as if to slow the beating of her heart.

Anne did a mental calculation. Mrs. Enke must be over sixty. Was caring for Fairlawn becoming a burden for her? Anne would have to find a way to help her. But first she had to deal with the visitor.

"Mr. Biddle has come to call."

Anne looked down at her dress. She couldn't greet visitors, even someone who had been almost part of the family like Philip Biddle, in something so wrinkled.

"Would you show him to the parlor?" she asked Mrs. Enke. "And perhaps make some tea. I'll be there in a few minutes."

"Uncle Philip, this is a surprise," Anne said ten minutes later. Though her hair was hastily twisted into a chignon instead of being arranged in her usual pompadour, she was wearing a pale blue dress that bore not a single wrinkle.

The former banker rose from the settee and took her hand in his. Tall and thin with white hair and pale blue eyes, Philip Biddle had been part of Anne's life for as long as she could remember. Other than the Harrods, he and the man she called Uncle Ralph had been the only people in town who had stood by her father after his investment advice had proven faulty and the companies that had appeared to be so promising on paper had defaulted on their loans, destroying hopes along with fortunes. Though his losses had been larger than any of the other investors', it had been John Moreland who had taken all of the blame and who'd been ostracized by most of his former friends.

Philip smiled. "A pleasant surprise, I hope." It was surely Anne's imagination that he held her hand longer than normal.

"Of course it is. You're always welcome at Fairlawn." Anne wouldn't forget that Philip and Ralph had been among the first to offer help after the fire.

As she took a seat on the other side of the fireplace, Philip nodded. "I wanted to come for a visit as soon as I heard you were back, but I thought I should give you some time to settle in."

Though his smile was warm, something in Philip's eyes made Anne wonder if he had heard about her plans for the nursery. She doubted he would approve any more than Charles had, whereas Rob . . . Anne gave herself a mental shake. She didn't understand why thoughts of Rob filled her days. Everything, it seemed, reminded her of him.

She focused her attention on her guest, giving Philip her warmest smile. "Jane will be sorry she missed you." Each day it seemed that Jane's morning rides lasted longer. Though she claimed she was simply exercising Susannah's horses, Anne wasn't so certain. Jane had been different since they'd returned, and it was difficult to attribute that difference to long horse rides. Anne bit the inside of her cheek. How rude she was, letting her attention wander.

Apparently unaware of the directions her thoughts had been taking, Philip leaned forward. "I came to visit you, my dear, not your sister. A man gets lonely living alone. He needs the sight of a pretty girl to brighten his days."

Though Philip had been a widower for some years, Anne suspected that the sorrow never disappeared. "You and Aunt Rosemary were always so kind to us when we were growing up. I hope you know you're welcome here anytime you need companionship."

Philip's lips turned up ever so slightly. "Oh, my dear, I must caution you against extending invitations you might regret. I'm afraid that I'm lonely most days."

"You must miss Aunt Rosemary very much." Anne refilled Philip's cup and offered him another of Mrs. Enke's lemon muffins.

"I do." He nodded as he dropped a sugar cube into his tea and began to stir it. "I miss your parents, too. But seeing you brings them closer." He reached over and touched Anne's hand. "You look so much like your mother."

I do? Anne could not hide her surprise. No one had ever told her that, and she saw no resemblance when she looked in the mirror. "You think so, Uncle Philip?"

"Indeed. But please don't call me Uncle Philip any longer. Surely you've passed the age where a courtesy title is necessary."

Anne nodded slowly, still mulling the fact that someone who'd known Mama when she was Anne's age believed there was a resemblance. "It's simply that I've always thought of you as an uncle," she told Philip. "It's the same with Uncle Ralph. I always considered both of you part of the family, even though we have no blood ties."

Philip's lips tightened, and she saw him clench his right hand. "Be careful, my dear," he said in a voice that seemed tinged with anger. "Ralph Chambers is not a man to be trusted. He's given more than one person bad advice."

Anne walked from one table to the next, moving one chair forward an inch, another back a few millimeters. It was silly. The moment the children arrived, the chairs would be moved again, some of them probably toppling over as the eager youngsters grabbed them. There was no need to re-arrange anything, but Anne couldn't help it. She needed to do something while she waited for the first child to arrive.

The day she had dreamt about for so long had finally come, and what a beautiful day it promised to be! The long heat wave had broken, and the air now bore the faint tinge of early autumn. Though it had rained two days earlier, the puddles had dried and the children would be able to play on the grass. Everything was ready. Including Anne.

Unable to sleep more than a few minutes at a time, she had arrived at the nursery early this morning, turning on the electric lights an hour before the official opening time. Of course no one had come that early, but now as the sun began to rise, they would start to arrive. She wondered who would be first. Would it be a little boy or a girl or maybe one of each?

They should be arriving soon. Anne walked to the Dutch door, opening the top of it. That looked more welcoming than a closed door. Now there could be no doubt that the nursery was open. She peered down the street. Though there were pupils scam-pering toward the schoolhouse, there were no mothers leading small children. Surely they'd come soon. Otherwise, the mothers would be late for their shift at the mill.

An hour later Anne sank into the rocking chair. There was no question about it. The morning shift had started; school was in session; the street was empty, and so was the nursery. Charles had been right. Anne's dream had turned into a nightmare. All that planning, all that work, and no one had come. Though she had thought there might be only a few children the first day, she had never considered that her nursery would be completely empty.

"Good morning."

Anne looked up as Rob entered the room, a smile on his face, one hand behind his back.

She tried to return the smile, but her lips refused to curve. "It would be a better morning if there were children here." Anne gestured toward the carefully arranged tables, the games that she'd laid out on the floor, the books that were waiting to be read. "I don't understand it, Rob. I put flyers everywhere. I told all the shopkeepers about the nursery. Where are the children?"

"They'll come." His voice held a confidence Anne wished she shared. She'd been so certain that her plan was a good one, but the empty room mocked that certainty.

Rob closed the bottom half of the door. "This is a new idea for Hidden Falls. It's a change. Anne, surely you know that it takes some people awhile to adjust to change, even good change."

Anne nodded slowly, remembering how she'd resisted some of the changes she'd found on her return.

"Meanwhile," Rob said, "I brought something I thought you might like." He extended the hand that he'd held behind his back and gave her an oddly shaped package wrapped in brown paper.

A gift! He continued to surprise her. Rob had helped in so many ways, and now this. "Oh, Rob!" Anne gasped with pleasure as she unwrapped the package. Inside was a wooden figure of a child seated on a carousel horse. The fine details left no doubt of who had carved and painted it. "It's beautiful!" Anne touched the child's face, marveling at the way Rob had captured the little girl's sense of wonder. "She looks so happy."

The breeze stirred the leaves on the old elm tree in front of the house, their rustling reminding Anne that autumn was coming. She wasn't sure whether it was the season's changing that made Rob pensive. All Anne knew was that he was staring outside, his face once more solemn.

"Childhood should be a happy time," he said at last. "We grow up all too soon." The sadness that Anne had heard in his voice whenever he spoke of childhood colored his words and made her wish there were something she could do to assuage his pain. Perhaps happy thoughts would help to chase the sorrow.

"One of my earliest memories is my mother pushing Jane and me on the swing in our backyard," Anne said, tracing the wooden child's figure. "Then one night when I couldn't sleep, I looked outside and saw Mama sitting on the swing with my father pushing her. I was so surprised. I didn't know that grownups played."

As Anne had hoped, the shadows that had haunted Rob's eyes were gone. "Isn't it a shame that we don't take the time to play? I never really thought about it, but maybe that's why I carve carousel horses — to give people an excuse to play." Rob walked to the back of the room and gazed out the window. "That oak tree would be the perfect place to hang a swing."

A swing for the children. What a wonderful idea! Anne joined Rob at the window, her gloomy mood dissipating. Though she had wanted to cheer him, his simple suggestion had reminded her to keep her dream alive, to find a way to bring children to the nursery. "You're right; it is the perfect spot." Once the children started coming, she'd find rope and a board and would make a swing. "Thanks, Rob." For the idea of a swing, for the carved figure, for so much else.

Anne looked at him and smiled. As he returned the smile, his eyes crinkling, she took a deep breath. *Why was it that he seemed so familiar?*

Mrs. Enke had outdone herself. Though normally supper was a casual meal, frequently little more than soup and one of her crusty breads, today she had prepared a collation of sliced meats and cheeses, adding the deviled eggs that she knew Anne particularly liked. Jane appeared to have been a co-conspirator, for there was freshly squeezed lemonade in addition to iced tea. Only Jane knew that Anne had developed a taste for lemonade during their stay in Switzerland. When Anne saw that the table was set for four, she realized that Charles and Susannah were joining them. Everyone, it seemed, wanted to celebrate Anne's first day at the nursery. Everyone, that is, except Anne.

"You know we're anxious to hear all about it," Susannah said as she passed the butter. "How was opening day?"

There was no point in mincing words. "It was a failure."

Though Jane gasped, it was Charles who breached the sudden silence. "Why do you say that?"

"Because no one came. Not one mother brought her child." Anne looked from Charles to Susannah then to Jane. They were her family. More than anyone except Rob, they understood how much the nursery meant to her. They wouldn't judge; they wouldn't condemn. Anne knew that. It shouldn't have hurt so much to pronounce those words, admitting that she had failed, but it did.

"That's awful!" Jane cut her meat with more force than necessary, a sure sign that she was angry.

Anne's anger had faded. Now all she felt was sorrow. "There's nothing more I can do. I can't very well drag children in off the street." She took a sip of lemonade, then turned to her sister-in-law. "When will you let me see some of your paintings?" Though Charles had told Anne of his wife's artistic talent, none of her paintings were on display at Pleasant Hill.

"It's gracious of you to ask." Susannah's little smile told Anne that she recognized a deliberate change of topic. "But your nursery is more important than my painting. There must be a way to encourage people to bring their children."

A bird fluttered by the long windows, its wings touching the glass for an instant before it realized the danger and flew away.

"I suspect folks are afraid." It was one of the things Anne had considered during the long day with only Rob's carving for company. Though she had known it was unlikely that a mother would bring her child after the noon meal, Anne was determined to keep her nursery open, and that had given her plenty of time to think. "I probably would be scared too. After all, they know their neighbors or whoever's caring for the children now. I'm a stranger."

Jane's frown was as uncharacteristic as her extended absences. "It's worse than that, Anne. You're someone from the hill."

Before Anne could respond, her brother raised his voice. "Now you're sounding like Matt." Despite their mother's training, Charles pointed his butter knife at Jane.

She refused to back down. "I'm simply telling you how we're viewed. You can say all you want about superior working conditions, but the fact is, they work for us, and they know that our profits are greater than their wages. Why should they trust us?"

"All that may be true," Susannah said, her tone that of a peacemaker, "but it isn't helping us solve the problem of Anne's empty nursery." She turned to her husband. "Isn't there anything you can do?"

"If you believe Jane, no."

Jane tossed her napkin onto the table. "Well, I can do something." She rose and walked toward the door. "And I will."

The next morning, Anne had no sooner switched on the lights than a woman knocked at the door. She held an infant in one arm, and a small boy clung to her other hand.

" 'Morning, ma'am," the woman said. "This here's Jamie and Joseph," she said, nodding toward the baby and the toddler. "Mr. Matt told me I should bring 'em here."

Anne opened the door and ushered them inside, saying a silent thank you to her sister. Jane, she was certain, had enlisted Matt Wagner's help in allaying the mill workers' fears.

"This here's a mighty pretty place," the woman, who had introduced herself as Mrs. Baker, said as she looked around the room with its perfectly arranged furniture. "You sure my young 'uns won't be no trouble for you?"

Anne led the older child to a pile of brightly colored toys, then reached for the infant. "I love children, Mrs. Baker. That's why I opened the nursery."

The woman's hesitation was palpable, and for an instant Anne was afraid she would snatch up her children and flee. But Mrs. Baker said only, "Iff'n you're sure . . ."

"I am."

By the end of the day, Anne was sure of only two things: that caring for children was far more work than she had dreamed possible and that she had never had so much fun in her whole life.

"It looks like you can use some help." Rob opened the door, grinning when he saw the overturned tables and the wooden blocks that had been flung in all directions.

"Who would have thought two children could make such a mess?" Anne asked as she bent to retrieve a rubber ball that had gotten lodged under one of the cribs.

"Perhaps they're simply getting used to a new place."

"Perhaps. I'll cling to that hope."

Rob up righted a table and arranged the chairs next to it. "Are you having second thoughts?"

"No!" Anne put down the bag of toys and looked at Rob. "It was wonderful. The time went so fast, and I felt as if I was . . ." She paused for a second, searching for the correct word. "Alive," she said at last.

"You always looked alive to me," Rob teased.

"Oh, Rob, you know what I mean. How do you feel when a horse is complete, and it turned out exactly the way you knew it would?"

He moved another set of chairs. "Like I could scale the highest mountain and not even be out of breath."

"Alive!"

"You're right: alive."

The sun was close to setting when Rob left the workshop. Though he could work under artificial light, tonight he was too restless to trust himself with a gouge or paintbrush. He settled his hat on his head and turned right onto River Road, heading toward the falls that had given the town its name.

Alive. What a strange way to describe his feelings, and yet Anne was right. There was an almost unbelievable sense of satisfaction when a horse was finished. No matter how many animals he created, each one was special, and when each was complete, he experienced that same elation. Rob had never thought he would find anything that could compare to it. But now . . .

He quickened his pace, wanting to reach the falls before dusk obscured the cataract. The falls had always been the place he'd come when he wanted to think, and tonight he needed to do just that.

So much had changed. When he had first arrived in Hidden Falls, he had thought it would be nothing more than a stopping place, a temporary home. Unlike many of the other carousel carvers who had permanent factories, Rob had envisioned his future as an itinerant carver. He and his assistants would travel from site to site, working directly with their clients. Each carousel would bring them new adventures and allow them to explore new parts of the country. It was an ideal life for three single men, and for Rob there was the additional advantage that one of the towns might be the one he sought, the one where Edith lived.

Rob turned onto the path that led to the falls. Though the shrubs and trees obscured the river, there was no disguising the sound of the torrent. He knew that when he descended halfway, he'd reach the break in the trees and the falls would no longer be hidden. No matter how many times he'd seen the falls, they'd never failed to thrill him, but tonight he found his feet moving mechanically while his thoughts whirled.

He had relished the idea of being an itinerant carver; now it was different. Now Rob could picture himself staying in one place. *Oh, why mince words?* He could envision staying in Hidden Falls. When he had told the man who was handling the sale of the Brickers' house that he was thinking about settling down, the story had been a ruse. But as he'd pronounced the words, Rob had realized that they were true. He wanted to settle down, not just anywhere but here in Hidden Falls.

He could imagine himself buying a small house with an outbuilding for a workshop. Mark and Luke would have space above the workshop, while he lived in the house with his wife.

Wife? Rob stopped abruptly, his boots sliding on the muddy path. *Where on earth had that thought come from?* He blinked in confusion, then resumed his pace. He couldn't settle down. He couldn't consider marriage. No, indeed. It wasn't simply that he couldn't afford a wife — and, at this point, he could not. When he married — if he married — he needed to be able to give his wife all of his time, all of his attention. That was the problem. He couldn't do that now. There was no way he could give a wife what she deserved until he found Edith, and finding Edith was beginning to feel like an impossible dream. There had been so many leads, so many letters, so many dead ends. It was almost as if his sister had vanished from the earth.

Rob had reached the break in the trees. He leaned against the low railing, staring at the water. The sight of endless water, the sound of the rushing torrent had always brought him a sense of calm. Not tonight. Tonight his thoughts were more turbulent than the water at the cataract's base, swirling around rocks, splashing on the river banks.

He needed to find Edith. Rob knew that as surely as he knew that the falls would continue to delight generations of Hidden Falls' residents long after he was gone. Then why, oh why, did he keep picturing himself with a wife, a wife who looked suspiciously like Anne Moreland?

Rob closed his eyes, trying to block the image. Anne wasn't for him. He knew that. She was as close to high society as Hidden Falls had, while he was nothing more than a hired laborer. She was beautiful and educated and when she married, it would be someone from her social circle, someone who could give her the luxuries that she deserved, someone like Brad Harrod.

Clenching his fists, Rob headed back up the path. For the first time, the beauty of the falls had failed to soothe him. Instead, the water seemed to mock him, telling him his dream could be swept away as easily as the twigs that tumbled over the precipice, reminding him that he needed to keep himself grounded in reality. Reality was that he and Anne were friends, nothing more. No matter what he might dream, he had to remember that.

CHAPTER FIVE

"You look tired." It was the end of the day, and Rob was helping Anne restore some semblance of order in the nursery. They had fallen into a routine. At first, he had come only to escort her home, but after he had seen the jumble of toys and overturned chairs, he had started arriving earlier and helping with the cleanup. Though Anne worried that she was taking time away from Rob's carving, her protests were almost perfunctory. The truth was, she enjoyed Rob's company, and their walks home were the highlight of her days. She'd regale him with tales of the children's shenanigans, while he'd explain some of the finer points of carving.

"I am tired," Anne admitted. "But I'm also happy." She slid another chair into place, then looked up at Rob. His golden hair was mussed, a combination of the September breeze and the fact that he had been too busy to visit the barber. "Another mother came today. She brought me three more children."

"How many do you have now?"

"Twelve." Anne didn't try to hide her satisfaction. "The nursery is full!" It had taken two weeks, but she had made her dream come true. And if twelve children's antics had exhausted her, well . . . that was the reality part of the dream.

"This calls for a celebration." Rob stroked his chin, the picture of a contemplative man. "Champagne is traditional, but I don't have any." A frown accompanied his words. "Flowers would be good, but I'd have to cut them from your garden." He was silent for a second. Then a grin lit his face. "There's only one thing to do." Rob started humming a Strauss waltz. Bowing as if he were at a formal party, he asked, "May I have the honor of this dance, Miss Moreland?"

"Here?" Anne couldn't believe that he was serious. They weren't dressed for dancing; they had no music, and even with the furniture once more arranged, there wasn't enough room for a couple to dance.

Rob looked around the room, as if seeing its shortcomings for the first time. "Outside, then." Without waiting for her assent, he took Anne's hand and led her into the backyard, then drew her into his arms.

Anne had danced dozens of times before. There had been lessons with the dancing instructor her mother had hired and practice sessions with a reluctant Charles as her partner. And then there had been the formal dances themselves. Elegant gowns, soft kid slippers, polished floors, the scent of flowers, a perfectly tuned orchestra. She had none of those today. Instead, she wore a simple dress, sorely wrinkled from playing with the children, and sturdy boots as she and Rob glided across newly mown grass, accompanied only by his humming.

Perhaps it should have felt awkward or even a bit ridiculous. Instead, Anne could not remember anything that had felt this good. The faint odor of paint clung to Rob, and she glimpsed a bit of sawdust in his hair. It didn't matter. All that mattered was the pleasure of being in Rob's arms, matching her steps to his as they waltzed across the grass. Anne's mother would have shuddered at the impropriety of her daughter dancing in full view of any passerby. Anne didn't care. For a few moments as Rob held her in his arms, she felt cherished and protected, and if her heart beat faster than a mere waltz warranted, that was all right too.

"What fun!" she said when Rob stopped humming and made another bow.

"Even more fun than riding a merry-go-round."

It was a statement, not a question, but Anne couldn't agree. "I'm not sure about that. It's been years since I rode one." She gathered her bag, closed the nursery door and once more matched her steps to Rob's. This time, though, they were merely walking, heading home as they did each day. *It was unfair,* Anne mused, *that they couldn't waltz all the way to Fairlawn. Wouldn't that fuel the rumor mill?*

She and Rob turned right onto Bridge Street and passed the park, stopping as they did each day to check the progress. Workers had already constructed the platform that would support the carousel once it was moved, and it appeared that little had occurred today. "When will the carousel be finished?"

"Less than a week now." Rob's voice held the same satisfaction that Anne's had when she had told him the nursery was full. "The engine and the cranks were delivered today, and we'll assemble them tomorrow. After that, all that's left is the final painting of two animals." Anne knew that Mark and Luke applied four coats of primer before they began the detailed color painting.

"Wonderful! I am so anxious." Since Charles had decreed that Anne couldn't see the carousel as it was being assembled, Rob had erected a wooden screen in front of the site where it would first be placed. Anne had seen pieces being carried there and had heard saws and hammers. Each day had heightened her anticipation, although her eagerness to see the finished carousel was tinged with regret. As wonderful as it would be to ride the merry-go-round, once it was completed, Rob would have no reason to remain in Hidden Falls, and that distressed Anne more than she cared to admit.

"What comes next?" she asked.

Rob shrugged his shoulders. "I'm not sure. Two men have expressed an interest in having me build carousels for them, but nothing is definite."

Anne blinked as she realized she'd been handed the key to a puzzle. That's why Rob had written all those letters. He'd been seeking future work. Why hadn't Anne thought of that when Jane had mentioned how many missives Rob sent?

"I wish I could help you." *And I wish you didn't have to leave Hidden Falls.*

"It's good to see you again, Anne." As she gestured toward the settee, the portly attorney took a seat. Anne couldn't help contrasting him with the other man who had sat there only a few weeks before. While Philip was tall and thin with white hair, Ralph Chambers was of only medium height but more than medium weight. His gray hair was thick, as were the lenses in his spectacles. "You're more beautiful than ever," the man who had been her father's lawyer and one of his closest friends said.

It was a lie, a polite one, perhaps, but a lie nonetheless. "I never thought you were a flatterer, Uncle Ralph." Anne looked in the mirror each day, and she knew what she saw wasn't beauty. Jane was beautiful; she was not.

Ralph shook his head, waiting until Mrs. Enke had laid the tea tray on the table before he continued. "It's nothing but the truth, Anne. You and Jane were beautiful girls, but when I look at you now, I see something more. If I were a poet, I'd say you were glowing."

"You're embarrassing me." Anne added two lumps of sugar to the tea cup, then handed it to her guest.

"I didn't mean to. It's simply that I was surprised at how much you resemble your mother."

Anne poured herself a cup, then looked up. "Uncle Philip said that, too."

"It's true." Ralph bit into one of the small sandwiches, chewing thoughtfully. When he spoke, his voice was soft, almost as if he didn't intend for Anne to hear his words. "Your mother was the most beautiful woman in Hidden Falls. All of us men were in love with her and more than a little envious of your father when he was the one who captured her heart."

He had said "us men." "Even you?" Though Ralph had been a frequent visitor to Fairlawn, Anne had never had the slightest inkling that he regarded her mother as more than a friend.

His smile was bittersweet. "Oh, yes, my dear. Even I." He took another swallow of tea, placing the cup carefully back on the saucer before he continued. "Your mother was the reason I never married. I wasn't willing to settle for second best."

Anne didn't know what to say. She and Jane had speculated on Ralph's single state and Jane had once suggested that he had lost a love, but never had they considered that his lost love might be their own mother.

As if he sensed her discomfort, Ralph said briskly, "I'm certain you didn't invite me here to reminisce about unrequited love. Is there something I can do to help you?"

Anne nodded, once more on solid ground. "I wanted your advice." Though Philip had cautioned her against taking Ralph's advice, Papa had trusted him. That was the only recommendation Anne needed. She offered Ralph a plate of gingerbread. "Have you met Rob Ludlow?" When Ralph nodded, Anne continued. "He's wonderfully talented but needs help with the more mundane aspects of being an entrepreneur. Do you have any suggestions?"

An hour and three pages of notes later, Anne showed her guest to the front door. How glad she was she had invited him!

"You're back early." Anne flashed a smile at her sister, wondering whether the rain was what had curtailed Jane's morning ride. Though it appeared to be lessening, the patter of raindrops against the window was still steady.

Jane nodded and helped herself to a piece of gingerbread. "And you had a visitor."

"Uncle Ralph. I asked him to come, because I wanted to talk to him about setting up a business."

"Your own?" Jane reached for the teapot and a clean cup.

"No, Rob's."

A raised eyebrow greeted Anne's statement. "I see." Jane was silent for a second. "Did he have good advice?"

Anne nodded. "But he also told me something I hadn't known. You were right, Jane." She paused for dramatic effect. "The reason Uncle Ralph never married was that he lost the woman he loved. I learned who she was."

When Anne did not continue, Jane laid down her teacup and glared at her sister. "Are you going to reveal the identity of this mystery woman?" she demanded.

"If you tell me where you go each morning." Anne felt as if she were a schoolgirl again, trading secrets with her sister. It had been years since they'd done that, but — oh! — how good it felt. If only Jane would play along.

The indecision on Jane's face was almost comical. Anne could see her warring thoughts as clearly as if they were spoken.

"I visit friends." It was an answer, but it wasn't good enough for Anne.

"Matt Wagner?" That would explain both Jane's secrecy and the fact that she had been able to enlist his help with the nursery.

Her reluctance obvious, Jane nodded. "Among others."

"I see." It was Anne's turn to raise an eyebrow and give her sister a knowing glance.

"And now that I've satisfied your curiosity, sister dear, tell me who it is that Uncle Ralph loves."

"Mama."

Anne watched Jane's eyes widen. She was silent for a moment before she said, "It makes sense. That also explains why Uncle Ralph never left Hidden Falls, even though he could have had a career with one of the big New York or Philadelphia law firms."

Anne nodded. It was like old times. She and Jane would remember different things, and together they would be able to reconstruct a scene. "Uncle Ralph said all the men were in love with Mama." As she pronounced the words, Anne realized she might have a piece to another puzzle. "Do you suppose Uncle Philip was one of them?"

"I wouldn't be surprised." Jane poured herself another cup of tea. "There were times when I caught him staring at Mama the way Charles looks at Susannah. I asked Mama about it once, and she told me I must have been mistaken. Now I wonder."

"If they were rivals, that might explain why Ralph and Philip don't seem to like each other." It would also explain the disparaging remarks that Philip continued to make about Ralph.

Jane was pensive. "But they were both friends with Papa. Doesn't that seem strange?"

It did. Anne realized that while she might have answered one question, another one had been raised.

"Oh, Susannah, these are incredible!" Anne walked around the square tower room that her sister-in-law used as a studio, studying the paintings that were casually propped against the walls. Although she had seen the scenes that Susannah had painted for the carousel rounding boards, this was the first time Anne had viewed her sister-in-law's primary work, and she wanted to savor the experience. It wasn't difficult. Susannah's painting was different from the art Anne had seen in museums. Her brush strokes were bolder, her use of color more innovative. But what distinguished Susannah's canvases from the others was the emotion that seemed to leap from them.

"I think this is my favorite," Anne said, pointing to a picture of a mythological creature emerging from a forest. The half-man, half-horse looked strangely familiar.

"It's my favorite, too," Susannah admitted. "This was the first painting I did after I arrived in Hidden Falls. I called it 'Promise of Spring'."

Anne looked more closely at the figure. "Is it my imagination, or does the centaur look like my brother?"

A peal of laughter greeted her question. "I'm afraid so." Susannah pointed to another canvas, telling Anne to study the man's features. "I should have realized that I was in love with Charles when his face started appearing in every one of my paintings, but I was engaged to someone else at the time, so I kept denying it."

Anne had heard only the broadest outline of her brother's romance, but she couldn't help asking, "Did you know that you loved him when you went to Paris?" If she had, Anne wondered how Susannah had been able to bear leaving him. Anne dreaded the thought that Rob would soon leave, and she wasn't in love with him. Of course she wasn't.

Susannah nodded. "I'll admit that I had second thoughts, but Charles insisted that I go. He knew that studying art from one of the masters in Paris was my dream, and he

106

wanted to make certain that dream came true."

"It did, didn't it?"

To Anne's surprise, Susannah looked uncomfortable with the question. "The dream changed once I arrived in Paris. Being there was wonderful, and I learned a lot about painting. But what I realized was that my dream was living here in Hidden Falls as Charles's wife." She straightened one of the paintings. "What about you, Anne? What are your dreams, other than opening the nursery?"

As quickly as a vision of Rob pushing a child on a swing flitted across Anne's mind, she dismissed it. Rob was kind, and he was a good friend, but he'd never love her the way Charles loved Susannah. A man like Rob who created beauty wouldn't want a wife who — no matter what Ralph and Philip said — was no longer beautiful. He would seek a woman who was as perfect as he was. It wasn't simply her lack of beauty. Rob wouldn't want a woman who had failed as Anne had.

"I don't know," Anne said at last. "I'm not sure we Morelands have dreams."

"Of course you do. You simply aren't admitting them. Charles didn't at first."

Could Susannah be right? Anne didn't

think so. "As much as he loves you, I can't imagine that Charles's dream is running the mill."

"I'm certain it wasn't. It was guilt that brought him back here after the fire."

"Guilt?" Anne stared at her sister-in-law. "What do you mean?" There was no reason on earth why Charles should feel guilt. It was Anne who bore the burden of culpability. She was the only one who could have saved their parents.

Susannah's lovely brown eyes were serious as she faced Anne. "Charles blamed himself for the fire, even after he learned that Brian O'Toole set it."

Anne's breath escaped with a whoosh, and her legs turned to rubber. She sank onto the room's one chair. "You're going too fast for me, Susannah. I thought that the fire was an accident, a horrible, horrible accident."

Susannah knelt next to Anne, chafing her hand between both of hers to warm it. "I imagine everyone thought that, but the insurance investigator found evidence of arson."

Arson? What other secrets had Charles been keeping? "Brian caused the fire?" Anne was still trying to absorb Susannah's revelations. "What possible reason could he have?"

Anne remembered the man who had been their horse trainer. Other than an unfortunate fondness for whiskey, he'd been an exemplary trainer, able to turn even the most difficult horses into ideal mounts. That gentle man had killed her parents? It couldn't be true. Anne had heard that Brian had died in an accident a couple months earlier. Since he could not longer defend himself, had someone turned him into a convenient scapegoat?

"Why would Brian want to kill my parents?" she asked Susannah.

"As I understand it, he had a grudge against your father for firing him."

Anne knew how much her father had regretted having to let Brian go. She also knew that he had had no choice. "Brian was drunk. He had endangered the horses."

Susannah nodded. She'd obviously heard that part of the story. "I know, but sometimes it's easier to blame someone else than to accept responsibility."

"That may be true," Anne agreed, although she found it difficult to picture Brian O'Toole as an arsonist. "That doesn't explain why Charles blamed himself."

Susannah took a deep breath, and Anne

had the feeling she was trying to choose her words carefully. "Apparently he had an argument with your father that day. That's why he left so abruptly. Charles thought if he'd stayed here, he could have prevented the fire."

"That's ridiculous!" The words burst forth, seemingly of their own volition. Anne couldn't believe that Charles thought he had any culpability. Surely he knew who was to blame for their parents' deaths. "I'm the one who's guilty." Anne gripped Susannah's hand so tightly that her own knuckles turned white. "If I had smelled the smoke sooner, I could have saved my parents."

Though Anne expected to see revulsion on Susannah's face, instead she saw tears of compassion in her sister-in-law's eyes. "Do you truly believe that?"

Anne nodded. Though she had told no one — not even Jane — she knew the role she had played in the tragedy.

Susannah tugged her hand loose, then wrapped her arms around Anne. "Oh, Anne, what a horrible burden you've been carrying. It's not true, though. You couldn't have saved them. The fire moved too fast." Though her voice was heavy with emotion, Susannah spoke as if she were presenting facts to a jury. "Dr. Kellogg told Charles

110

they died within a minute. It would have taken you that long just to run from their room to yours. You couldn't have saved them," she repeated.

Anne stared at Susannah. Was it possible? "I wish I could believe that."

Susannah hugged her again. "Believe it."

"It's true." Hidden Falls' only physician leaned across the desk to emphasize his words. Though Anne had wanted to believe Susannah, she had needed to hear the words directly from Dr. Kellogg. That was the reason she had rushed to his office as soon as she'd closed the nursery instead of walking home with Rob.

The visit hadn't gone the way she'd expected. The doctor had taken one look at Anne and, without asking why she had come, had prescribed a sleeping draft. It was true that she was exhausted. Twelve children were more work than she'd dreamed possible, but that wasn't the reason she wanted to consult the doctor. When she'd explained that she had another concern, he had listened carefully, then nodded, echoing Susannah's words.

"Mrs. Moreland is correct." For a moment, Anne was confused before she realized that the doctor meant Susannah.

How odd to think of someone other than Mama being Mrs. Moreland! "No one could have saved them."

Anne knew it was only because she was so tired, but as Dr. Kellogg confirmed what Susannah had said, she felt tears prickle her eyelids. It was relief, mingled with the sadness that never seemed to fade.

"How foolish of me," the doctor continued. "I was so concerned with treating your burns that I never considered you might have other kinds of wounds." He had examined the Swiss doctors' work and had pronounced it little short of a miracle. "The scars on your face have healed well. I should have realized, though, that there were others. The invisible wounds are the hardest to cure." Dr. Kellogg frowned. "I wish I'd thought to say something about the fire's speed when I first started treating you."

Anne couldn't let him assume a burden of guilt. "You've helped me, more than you may ever know. Thank you, doctor." She kept her eyes on him, refusing to look at the wall behind him where two gas lamps provided the room's illumination. "Do you think I'll ever lose my fear of fire?" Ever since that night, even the smallest flame or the faintest hint of smoke had made Anne cringe in fear.

"Everyone should fear fire," the doctor said slowly.

"Even a candle's flame?" Anne knew the fear wasn't rational, but that didn't change the way she felt. She had directed Mrs. Enke to remove the silver candelabra that was a Moreland heirloom from the dining room, insisting that the electric light would be sufficient. Thank goodness Charles had electrified Fairlawn!

"Learning to overcome fear takes a long time," Dr. Kellogg said. "I saw the way you reacted to my gas lights. Even now, you won't look at the wall."

"I wouldn't have them in the nursery." Anne had been adamant about that. It was bad enough that she had to enter buildings where people burned candles or used gas lights. She was an adult. She knew the danger, and she could run. The children were different. Anne wouldn't risk their lives.

"I've heard good things about your nursery," the doctor said with a twinkle in his eye. Anne knew he was deliberately changing the subject, and she welcomed the diversion. "Every day at dinner, the nursery is all Bertha can talk about. I think my daughter wishes it had been her idea. She's at loose ends now that she's no longer working at the mercantile."

As Anne remembered how sensible Bertha Kellogg had always seemed in school, an idea began to form. Though she had come to the doctor's office for a different reason, Anne thought she might have found the solution to one of her problems.

"Do you think Bertha would want to work at the nursery?"

The doctor chuckled. "I think I can safely say that she'll accept before you've finished asking her."

He was right.

The sun would be setting within half an hour. Anne paced the floor of her room, wishing her brother would call. Tonight was the night. Tonight she would finally see the carousel. Tonight she would be able to ride it. If only the waiting would end. Charles's insistence on secrecy guaranteed that the completed carousel would be a surprise, but it also meant that Anne felt like a prisoner, confined to a room with drawn drapes while the final preparations were underway.

"Anne, Jane! We're ready!"

At last! Heedless of decorum, Anne ran down the stairs, grinning at Charles and Susannah. "I thought you'd never call." In honor of the occasion, she'd ordered a new dress. The royal blue silk might be more suited to a formal ball than to riding a merry-go-round, but Anne didn't care. Neither, it appeared, did Susannah. She was wearing a peach silk evening gown. The two women shared a conspiratorial smile, silently approving each other's attire.

Oblivious to the wordless communication, Charles looked behind Anne. "Where's Jane?"

"I don't know. She went on one of her mysterious errands." Though Anne suspected those errands involved Matt Wagner, she had no intention of telling Charles that.

Charles's lips thinned. "I can't believe your sister is so inconsiderate," he said, seeming not to remember that Jane was also his sister. "She knew that we planned to light the carousel as soon as the moon rose." Though Susannah put a calming hand on his arm, Charles shook his head. "We can't wait for her. She'll just have to miss it."

Anne tried not to mind that Jane wasn't here. The two of them had shared almost every experience of their lives, and Jane knew how much Anne was looking forward to the carousel's unveiling. What was so important that she couldn't wait an hour? If Anne's assumptions were correct, Jane spent every morning with Matt. Why did she have to be gone now?

But as Anne approached the carousel flanked by Charles and Susannah, her worries about Jane were momentarily forgotten, for standing there in front of the darkened merry-go-round was Rob, looking as if he had worries of his own. Though he was dressed more formally than normal, with a stiff high collar instead of the soft stocks that he preferred and a dark suit that highlighted his golden hair, there was no mistaking the furrows between his eyes.

"What's wrong?" Anne whispered the words, not wanting Charles and Susannah to overhear.

For a second, she thought Rob would not reply. Then he said, "I'm afraid you won't like it."

Though Anne knew that Rob's fears were unfounded, she also knew that most fears appeared irrational — even silly — to others. Look at her own phobia about candles. What she needed to do was to allay Rob's concerns. "Oh, Rob. I've seen all the animals save one, and they're beautiful. How can the finished product be anything less than magnificent?" Anne took his hand and led him back to where Charles and Susannah stood.

In the dim light of dusk, she could see the

outlines of the animals and the building that housed them, but the details were hidden, waiting for the moment when the moon began to rise. Rob had confided to Anne that Charles had urged him to have everything ready for tonight, since tonight was the full moon.

"He's convinced there's something special about a full moon," Rob had explained.

There had been a full moon the night of the fire. Perhaps Charles wanted to replace that association with a happier one. If so, Anne knew he'd chosen well. Surely the carousel would bring only happy memories.

As the sky darkened, Anne saw the glow on the horizon that heralded the moon. Soon. Soon she would see the carousel that Rob had created, the one that Charles had commissioned for her. Soon the music would begin and the painted ponies would revolve. Anne gripped Rob's hand tighter, almost not daring to breathe. She felt his pulse race and knew that he was as excited as she.

"Now!" Charles gave the command, and the lights were switched on.

Anne gasped. This merry-go-round was far different from the one she remembered. Not even her imagination had conjured anything so beautiful. Hundreds of white lights outlined the crown center and the sweeps, with still more circling the rounding board and illuminating the animals below. Though Anne knew that the rounding board had been illustrated with pictures depicting parts of Hidden Falls' history, she only glanced at the oil paintings Susannah had created. There would be time for that later. What mattered now were the animals Rob had carved.

They stood in two rows. Eight pairs of horses shared the platform with the elephants, bears, giraffes, and ostriches. Two by two, they circled the wooden platform, their brass poles waiting for eager riders to grasp them when the ride began. Individually, they were beautiful. Together they could only be described as breathtaking.

"Oh, Rob! This is even more magnificent than I dreamed." Anne walked toward the carousel, accepting Rob's assistance as she climbed onto the platform. Then slowly, as if she had all the time in the world, she moved from one row of animals to the next, touching each animal reverently. Though she had seen them before, there was something special, something almost magical, about seeing the carousel assembled. It was more than the addition of lights and brass poles. Now that they were together, though they bore the flamboyant colors Rob had told her were characteristic of the Coney Island style, the animals looked almost real. Anne sighed from pure pleasure. No gift she had ever received could compare to this.

And then she reached the one animal that Rob had not allowed her to see before tonight. Though it had been finished before she returned from Switzerland, he had kept it covered, telling her he wanted it to be a surprise. Anne knew that as the lead horse, it would be more elaborate than the others. She knew that this was the one animal that Rob, as the head carver, would sign. She knew that. What she didn't know was how different that horse would be from the others. While the others had traditional poses, this one was a stargazer, its head turned upward. While the others had painted manes, this one's was gilded. And this one alone had a small figure attached to its saddle. Anne knew that carvers called the small figures Chernis, after Salvatore Cernigliaro, the man who had first added one to a horse. She moved closer, and her heart skipped a beat when she identified this Cherni.

"Oh, Rob! It's my doll!" When Anne and Jane had grown too old to play with dolls, their mother had placed their favorite toys in a cabinet in her bedroom, announcing that she was saving them for her grandchildren. Anne had assumed that the contents of that cabinet had been destroyed along with so much else. It appeared she was wrong, for this figure was so close to the original that Rob must have used the doll itself as a model. Anne touched the tiny face, then stroked the carved hair. That was golden blond, as Annabelle's had been, and her gown was deep blue, the same color that Anne was wearing tonight. "She's perfect!" Like the whole carousel. Like Rob. Bending closer to read the letters that were painted on the doll's skirt, Anne gasped. Where she had expected to see Rob's signature, she found her own name.

"It's your carousel," he said softly.

Anne's heart was pounding so hard that she could barely breathe. "I have never had anything so beautiful." Though she and Jane and Charles had not lacked for possessions, nothing could match this. Anne stared at the carousel, humbled by its magnificence. "How can I thank you?" She turned her eyes back to Rob and smiled as she gazed at him.

The worry lines that had furrowed his brow were gone, and Rob's eyes twinkled as he said, "Thank Charles."

Charles. For a moment, Anne had forgotten that her brother and Susannah were still standing on the grass, waiting for her to complete her inspection. As she'd walked around the platform, her world had shrunk until it encompassed only the animals and Rob. But Charles, whose idea it had been, and Susannah, who had contributed her talent to its creation, were waiting patiently. Anne turned and smiled at them. "Thank you, Charles. You're the best of brothers."

He shrugged, as if commissioning a carousel was nothing extraordinary. "Are you ready to ride?"

"I wish Jane were here, but . . ." Before she could complete the sentence, Anne saw her sister approaching the carousel, a tall man at her side.

"Matt!" Anne heard the anger in her brother's voice. In a second he would order the man he considered an intruder to leave Fairlawn, and Jane would in all likelihood go with him.

"Please, Charles," Anne pleaded, "can't you let bygones be bygones for one night?"

When her brother started to shake his head, Susannah put her hand on her husband's arm, then touched his cheek. Charles's face softened. "All right. Let's ride." He gestured toward Jane and Matt, silently urging them to mount the platform.

For a second, Anne thought Matt would refuse, but then her sister smiled at him, and he returned her smile with one so tender that it touched Anne's heart. Jane had said she spent her mornings visiting friends. If those smiles were any indication, Matt and Jane were more than friends. No wonder she was being so secretive.

Charles and Susannah walked toward a row of giraffes, while Jane and Matt chose a pair of horses on the opposite side of the merry-go-round. Anne, knowing there was only animal she would ride, returned to the lead horse. Though he walked next to her, Anne sensed Rob's hesitation.

"I was hoping you'd ride with me," she said softly. Though she and Rob were only friends, this was a moment they had to share.

He grinned. "I was hoping you'd ask."

As he settled onto the horse next to her, Rob gave the signal. The Wurlitzer organ began to play, and the steam engine began to turn the cranks. Slowly at first but with increasing speed, the horses began to revolve. Around and around; up and down. Anne laughed with pure delight as she and Rob passed each other again and again, one moving up while the other moved down.

Was there anything on earth so wonderful?

Riding a carousel was even more magical than Anne remembered. The night her parents had rented a merry-go-round for her and Jane's birthday celebration had been wonderful, but tonight surpassed that. Tonight she was an adult, able to appreciate not just the beauty of the animals but all the work that had gone into creating them. Tonight she knew that life wasn't always perfect, and that made this moment all the more special, because it was perfect. Though it might never be repeated, this was a night she would never forget. No matter what the future brought, she would cherish this special night. Her family was once more together. She was riding the most beautiful carousel in the world, and . . . Why deny it? The others were important, but what made tonight truly special was having Rob at her side.

When the music ended and the carousel slowly spun to a stop, Anne waited for Rob to help her off the horse. "I want to ride them all," she announced.

"It's your night, princess." Charles gave Anne a fond smile as he and Susannah moved toward a pair of horses and the music began again. Half an hour later, the others had left and Anne and Rob were alone with the carousel. They had ridden each pair of animals, but Anne wanted one final ride on the lead horse. Her horse.

"This was the most wonderful day of my life," Anne said as the music ended and she slid off the horse.

Rob helped her descend from the platform, then switched off the lights. They stood silently for a moment, letting their eyes adjust to the darkness. The carousel was as silent as they, silhouetted against the full moon, yet Anne knew that if she closed her eyes, she could re-create the magic of the lights, the music, and Rob's magnificent painted ponies.

"I will never forget this day," she said fervently.

"Nor will I." Rob reached for Anne's hand. "It wasn't just you, Anne. This was the most wonderful day of my life too."

Anne understood. "It should be. It's not every day you get to see your first complete carousel in operation." She could only guess at the feelings Rob was experiencing, but she imagined that pride and satisfaction were at the forefront, as they should be.

An owl hooted, a nocturnal animal scurried through the grass, some night-blooming flowers perfumed the air. Rob laced his fingers through Anne's. "That's not the reason today was special." His voice was husky with an emotion she could not identify. All Anne knew was that whatever Rob was feeling, it was intense. She looked up at him, watching the moonlight illuminate those features that haunted so many of her dreams.

"It was you, Anne," he said softly. "You're what made today so wonderful."

Before she knew what he intended, Rob had drawn her into his arms. He touched her chin, tilting her face toward his, and slowly, ever so slowly, he lowered his lips to hers.

CHAPTER SIX

Something was wrong. Anne pulled the navy skirt from the wardrobe, then laid it on the bed next to her white shirtwaist. The clothing was a few years out of style but was perfectly adequate for cleaning the attic, which was what she had planned for this Saturday morning. She sighed as she reached for a pair of sturdy shoes. In the past, when she had felt like this, Anne had known the reason why. Too many days of relentless rain would cause this malaise; so, too, had some of the Swiss doctors' treatments. But this was different. There was neither a rain cloud nor a doctor in sight.

She ought to be happy. The nursery was full; she was no longer exhausted; the children all seemed content. No doubt about it, hiring Bertha Kellogg was one of the best things Anne had ever done. The children loved Bertha, and each day her assistant's pleasure at being part of the nursery seemed to increase. As for her own . . . she slid her arms into the waist and began to button it. To quote Shakespeare, there was the rub. That early feeling of exhilaration that she'd had when she'd opened the nursery had dissipated. Oh, she still felt satisfied with what she had accomplished. The nursery was something Hidden Falls needed, and the mothers as well as the children were vocal in their appreciation. Still, something was missing. Something important, and Anne had no idea what it was. All she knew was that her heart no longer quickened with anticipation when she approached the nursery each morning, and she no longer had that wonderful feeling of being alive that she'd once described to Rob.

Then there was Rob himself. If she lived to be a hundred, Anne doubted she would understand him. It had been over a week since the night he had kissed her, and — though she had seen him a dozen times since then — he had never once referred to it. From the way he acted, you would think that night had never happened. Perhaps he wished it hadn't. Anne had read about people getting swept up in the magic of a moment, saying and doing things they later regretted. Perhaps that was what had happened to Rob.

It was different for her — very, very different. Rob's kiss had been wonderful! It was the sweetest thing that had ever happened to her, and she never wanted to forget it. Anne's pulse raced each time she thought of how good it had felt to be held in Rob's arms, how the touch of his lips on hers had made her feel as if she were special, as if she were once again beautiful. If that wasn't magic, Anne didn't know what was. She dreamed of Rob and that magical moment every night, and memories of it brightened even the gloomiest of days. For Anne it had been an unforgettable evening. For Rob, it had meant nothing.

Anne stepped into the skirt and fastened the waistband, chiding herself for her foolishness. She should have known better. She should have known not to dream. Hadn't she told Susannah that Morelands didn't have dreams? Silly, silly Anne. She had known that Rob was simply being kind to her, that he would never view her as more than a friend. She had known better than to conjure a fantasy world, one that included happy endings. But for one moment, she had forgotten every piece of wisdom she had learned. For one moment, nothing had mattered but her and Rob. For one moment, she had let herself be swept away by the magic of his kiss. What a fool she was!

Anne brushed her hair with more force than necessary, as if she could brush away her silly dreams. She needed to face reality, and reality was that there were no happy endings for Anne Moreland. Perhaps scrubbing the attic floor would help. Her mother had always said that good, honest work was the cure for what ailed most people.

Anne was placing the last comb in her hair when Mrs. Enke knocked on the door, then poked her head inside. "Mr. Biddle is here to visit you."

Anne smiled. Maybe, just maybe, Philip could chase away her doldrums better than a mop and scrub brush.

"Good morning," she said only a minute later when she joined Philip in the front parlor. Though she wished it were Rob who had come to call, there was no reason to inflict her disappointment on the older man. "Would you like some tea or coffee?"

He shook his head. "Perhaps later. It's a beautiful morning, and I thought you might be willing to show me the carousel I've heard so much about." There was something in Philip's voice that made Anne think the carousel was only an excuse. That was ridiculous, almost as ridiculous as her dreams of Rob. Philip was not a man to prevaricate.

Anne led the way through the house and onto the south lawn. "You know we're going to move the carousel to the park," she said as, in deference to Philip's age, they walked slowly toward the platform. The ponies' vibrant colors shone in the light of day and their silver horseshoes sparkled. Anne smiled as she did every time she thought of the merry-go-round and the man who'd created it.

"That's generous of you, my dear." Philip drew Anne back to the present as he laid her hand on his arm, then covered it with his other hand. "You're a lovely young woman. Your parents would be proud if they could see you now." The words were kind; there was no reason why they should make Anne uncomfortable, and yet they did, just as the pressure of Philip's hand on hers made her want to squirm. Anne was relieved when they reached the carousel and she could disengage her hand to gesture toward the animals.

"I saw several of the horses a few months ago," Philip admitted. Though he and Anne stood next to the carousel, Philip gave the animals only a cursory glance. Instead, his gaze remained firmly fixed on Anne. "That carver did a fine job."

"He did, indeed." No matter what he felt for her, Rob was a supremely talented artist. His work would be a wonderful legacy for the town. "I can't wait to see the children's faces when they first ride it," Anne said, remembering her first ride and how she hadn't wanted it to end.

"Ah, yes, the children." Philip turned toward away from the merry-go-round. "Would you mind if we sat down?" He gestured toward the wrought iron bench that had once been inside the gazebo. When they were seated, Philip's lips curved in a wry smile. "I'm afraid, my dear, that I came here under slightly false pretenses. What I wanted was to talk to you about that nursery."

Anne tried not to flinch at either his tone or the fact that he hadn't referred to it as *her* nursery.

"I must be frank about this." Philip took her hand between both of his. "Your mother would have said the same thing if she were still here. My dear, it is unseemly for a gentlewoman like you to be caring for other women's children. You should marry and have children of your own."

Anger vied with the rules of courtesy her mother had instilled. *He means well,* Anne

131

told herself. *He's only trying to help.* She bit back her angry retort and said as mildly as she could, "Uncle Philip, you're beginning to sound like Charles."

Though she meant her comment to be chiding, Philip simply nodded. "I always knew Charles was a sensible young man. You should take his advice. And," Philip frowned slightly, "I thought I told you I dislike being called Uncle Philip."

"I'm sorry, Philip." It was surprisingly difficult to use his first name without the courtesy title. "The habits of a lifetime are hard to break." A flock of geese winging their way south filled the air with their honking. When they were gone, Anne took a deep breath. How she addressed Philip wasn't important; the nursery was. "It's fine for you and Charles to speak of marriage, but if you look around, you won't see a line of suitors knocking on my door. That's part of the reason I opened the nursery." Anne closed her eyes, trying to obliterate the image of herself holding a baby and smiling at a man who looked distinctly like Rob Ludlow. "One of the things I've known since the fire is that I shall never marry."

The older man could not conceal his shock. "Why on earth not?"

"Because no one would want me." Anne

touched her forehead. Despite the Swiss doctor's skill, scars remained at her hairline, and there were other scars on her throat and arms. Though the doctor had said they would fade with time, Anne knew how ugly they were.

"My dear Anne, you are mistaken." Philip tightened the grip on her hand. "Why . . ." He broke off the sentence, shaking his head as he muttered something that sounded like "too soon." His voice was once more strong as he said, "I wish Rosemary and I had been blessed with children. They would have made my life complete. You know, Anne, a man doesn't want to depart this earth without having left a legacy."

Anne looked at the carousel. It had been only a few minutes since she had thought of it as Rob and the Moreland family's legacy to the town. But Philip had a different definition of legacy.

Uncomfortable with the direction the conversation had taken, Anne rose, giving Philip no choice but to follow her. When he refused her offer of coffee and left Fairlawn, Anne felt oddly drained. Philip's disapproval of the nursery was not unexpected, but his insistence that she marry and his reference to his own legacy left her feeling unsettled. Though the attic needed cleaning, Anne needed something to keep her from dwelling on Philip's visit.

Almost without a conscious decision, her feet propelled her toward the workshop. When she reached the former stable, she found Rob busy sketching. There was no sign of Mark and Luke. "Do you mind if I look?" Rob might have chosen to forget the night they had kissed, but Anne knew he would offer her what he always had: friendship. He shook his head and spread out the paper so she could see the full figure.

Anne stared at it for a second, surprised. "A centaur?" Though the animal was clearly designed to be part of a merry-go-round, for it had a pole extending from its back, it was different from any carousel animal she had ever seen. Rob had told her that menagerie figures were normally either common barnyard animals or ones that could be seen in zoos. A centaur was neither. It existed only in mythology.

Rob nodded. "I saw a centaur in one of Susannah's paintings, and I couldn't stop thinking about it."

It was Anne's turn to nod. "Promise of Spring" had had that effect on her, too. "That painting is my favorite of Susannah's." Anne studied Rob's drawing again, intrigued by the design. Thoughts began to

134

whirl as she pictured the carousel on a platform, surrounded by other equally fantastical creatures. She looked up at Rob. "Have you considered making a whole carousel with mythological figures? You know, unicorns, griffins, and of course the centaur."

This time Rob shook his head. "This was just a whim. I thought that perhaps if I drew it, I'd stop thinking about Susannah's centaur."

It was, Anne reflected, a pity that she had no artistic talent. Perhaps if she did, she could draw Rob's face and then stop thinking of him.

"Did it work?" she asked.

Rob shook his head again. "I still want to carve it. But a whole carousel? Who would buy it?" Rob gestured toward the sketches of the Moreland carousel that still papered the walls. "Carousel owners will tell you that horses are the favorite animals. That's what people want to ride. If the carousel is a menagerie, the other animals," Rob pointed toward the elephant, "are the last ones to be chosen."

That might be true for ordinary carousels, the ones destined to be placed in a trolley park, but Anne had a different idea. While she had been waiting for Susannah to clean her brushes one day, Anne had leafed through several magazines, amazed at the variety. It was, Susannah had told her, the result of having professors as parents. "They were interested in everything," Susannah had said. Having seen their choice of periodicals, Anne couldn't disagree.

She touched the sketch of the centaur. "I read that the Mythological Society of America was having its centenary next year. There's going to be a big celebration in Philadelphia with hundreds of people coming from all over the country. What better way to celebrate than having a Ludlow carousel for all the attendees to ride?"

"It's a nice thought, Anne." Rob's skepticism was evident. "But just because you like carousels doesn't mean that everyone does. Why, the members of this Mythological Society have probably never ridden one."

Rob sounded as miserable as she had felt this morning. Though the conversation with Philip had only deepened her malaise, Anne's spirits had risen steadily since she'd entered the workshop. It was, she reflected, almost impossible to be unhappy near a carousel. And, of course, there was Rob. He was the most talented person she'd ever met. Seeing the results of his talent made her happy. That was the only reason she had come to the workshop. Of course it was.

"You're right," Anne conceded. "It's likely that people who spend their days reading aren't familiar with simple pleasures like merry-go-rounds. What if we changed that?" For several weeks, she had been searching for ways to help Rob become established as an independent carousel carver. "Charles knows a lot of people in New York, and he may even know someone who's part of this society. We could invite some of them to Hidden Falls to see the carousel."

"Do you truly believe they would come?" Rob's tone made it clear that he was convinced otherwise.

Anne did. "It won't just be the mythological people. We'll invite some of Charles's classmates and business associates — and their wives, of course. Charles can use the excuse of his own marriage and claim he wants them to meet Susannah." Anne warmed to the subject. "We'll make it a weekend event. The carousel will be part of it, but having them here will give Charles a chance to show off his new textiles, and Brad can promote the railroad. All of Hidden Falls could benefit."

Anne looked up at Rob, eager to see his reaction to her proposal. It was a good one; she knew it. But though Rob nodded, he said only, "I suppose." His lack of enthusiasm stung worse than the nettle patch she'd fallen into as a child. Feeling more than a little rebuffed, Anne returned to the house. Suddenly, scrubbing floors seemed like a good activity.

The day could not have been more perfect if she'd ordered it. Blue skies, an occasional puffy white cloud, the tang of autumn in the air. It was the ideal day for the unveiling of the carousel.

"Of course you're coming." Though Rob looked uncomfortable in his starched collar, Anne sensed that his discomfort was not caused by his effort at sartorial splendor but rather by the thought of being on the platform with her, Charles, Susannah, Jane, and the mayor. He had protested so vehemently that he should not be seated with what he called the dignitaries that Charles had appeared to waiver. Anne, however, remained adamant. "Hidden Falls wouldn't have a carousel if it weren't for you," she told Rob for what felt like the hundredth time. It wasn't simply that Anne believed Rob should receive public accolades for his work. That was part of it, but she also knew that the Hidden Falls paper would run a picture and, if luck was with her, that picture might be picked up by the news services. If that happened, it would be the priceless free advertising her father had advocated.

Though obviously chafing at his fate, Rob nodded. "Let's hope the ceremony doesn't take too long."

Charles chuckled as he entered the parlor. "You obviously haven't met our mayor if you think that's possible. We'll be there until dark."

Charles was right. When they reached the park and took their places on the platform, the mayor had already arrived and was greeting the townspeople. He was, Anne knew, running for reelection in a few months and appeared to view this as a golden opportunity to campaign.

By two o'clock, the designated time for the ceremony, the park was filled. Though there was a low murmur of conversation, most people were silent, staring at the red, white and blue tarps that covered the carousel. It had been Susannah's idea to drape the merry-go-round with special fabric made by the Moreland Mills.

"There will be more suspense if people can't see the horses right away," she explained, "and using fabric that they had a part in making will make them feel as if the carousel is really theirs." Anne wasn't certain Charles agreed, but since he rarely denied Susannah any of her wishes, the carousel was draped.

"Ladies and gentlemen." The mayor rose and began to address the crowd. Half an hour later, though the townspeople were visibly restless, he was still speaking. Anne knew that she was tired of listening to him, and she had the benefit of a chair. Everyone else was standing. How much longer would it be before boredom outweighed curiosity and people began to leave? How much longer would it be before someone fainted?

Anne took a deep breath. Her mother would have disapproved, if she had known what she was planning. Charles might chide her. Philip undoubtedly would. It didn't matter.

Anne rose and moved to stand next to the mayor. Though she said nothing, he was so startled by her appearance that he paused for a second. A second was all Anne needed.

"Thank you for your beautiful introduction, Mr. Mayor," Anne said in her sweetest voice. "And now, ladies and gentlemen, I would like to present the Moreland Carousel."

A dozen men had been waiting for those words. As Anne pronounced them, they tugged, releasing the tarps that had covered the merry-go-round. The brightly colored fabric drifted to the ground, revealing the elaborate pavilion and Rob's magnificent animals. A collective sigh burst forth from the crowd, and Anne heard a child cry, "Bootiful." It was indeed. A second later, the music started and the carousel began to revolve. Anne had suggested that they run it once with no riders so that everyone could enjoy the beauty before they formed a queue.

For the next several hours, she walked through the crowd, talking to the people she knew, introducing herself to others, watching them enjoying the carousel, taking pleasure from the smiles that she saw on their faces. Susannah was right. The merry-go-round was too special to be kept on the hill. It belonged to the people of Hidden Falls. It was perfect . . . almost. There was one flaw, and that flaw worried Anne more than a sore tooth. There had to be a solution.

Dusk had fallen before they stopped the carousel for the night and she and Charles and Susannah returned to Fairlawn. To Anne's surprise, Charles had said nothing about her interrupting the mayor, though Susannah had whispered her approval, saying, "Someone had to stop that windbag." As soon as the carousel had begun to revolve, the two of them had joined Anne, greeting townspeople and showing some of the children how to mount the animals.

Anne hadn't been surprised when Jane had gone in a different direction, saying only that she would meet them back at Fairlawn. It was Rob whose disappearance had surprised her. As soon as the speech was concluded and the carousel unveiled, he had climbed down from the platform, and Anne had lost sight of him. Where was he? Didn't he want to savor the pleasure of watching people enjoy his masterpiece? She had known he hadn't wanted the limelight of being on the platform, but she had thought he would have wanted to see his carousel in full operation. Mark and Luke seemed to be basking in the glory.

Charles and Susannah remained at Fairlawn for only a few minutes, and Jane had not yet returned, leaving Anne feeling strangely lonely. Normally she did not mind being alone, but tonight was not an ordinary night. Tonight she needed to be with Rob. There were no lights on at the workshop. Where was he? Anne told herself she was being foolish. Her problem could wait until tomorrow. But still she longed to see Rob, to share today's success with him and to ask if he would help her resolve the problem. Where was he?

Anne wandered through the house, then returned to the library. Perhaps a book would keep her from thinking about Rob. As she looked out the long French doors, she saw a figure walking toward the site of the old gazebo, the place where the carousel had resided for a few days. The man's head was bowed, his shoulders slumped as if in despair. There was no question of the man's identity, but why, oh why, did Rob feel that way?

Heedless of the damp grass that would ruin her shoes, Anne flung open the doors and ran toward Rob. "Is something wrong?" she asked without preamble. "You look sad." And that made her heart ache. Today should have been a joyous one for him, not one that depleted his energy and discouraged him.

Rob turned, and in the moonlight Anne could see the furrows between his eyes. "I'm not sad," he said, though his expression gave lie to his words. "It's simply that I planned for this day for so long, and now it's over. This is the end."

He was wrong, so very wrong. "This isn't the end. It's a wonderful beginning for the town. Just think of it, Rob. Charles and Susannah's grandchildren will enjoy the carousel you built."

"I suppose so." He kicked an acorn across the grass. "I don't mean to inflict my mood on you, Anne. This should be a happy day for you, and I don't want to spoil it. That's why I left the celebration when I did. It's simply that I'm feeling as if I'm lost at sea. I don't know what's coming next."

Anne could understand that. She had spent the better part of a year in Switzerland wondering what her future would be. But Rob was different. He had an undeniable talent. "You'll build another carousel."

"That was the plan," he agreed, his voice filled with sorrow, "but I don't have any orders yet. The two men who were interested decided not to go ahead with their projects. Oh, Anne, I hate the fact that when Mark and Luke ask where we're going next, I can't give them an answer."

Rob might not have given his assistants an answer, but he'd given Anne the perfect introduction to her problem and its solution. "I have an answer for you," she said. "I'd like you to build another carousel for me."

The crescent moon provided enough light that Anne could see the surprise on Rob's face. He shook his head. "That's a nice gesture, Anne, but you know as well as I do that Hidden Falls doesn't need more than one carousel."

"I beg to differ. I was watching the townspeople today as they rode it." She had been watching carefully, observing which animals were the favorites, smiling when she saw young girls racing toward the lead horse. That was when she had recognized the problem. "Everyone enjoyed the carousel except for the small children. Even with their parents holding them on the animals, they were afraid. Some of them cried; others simply clung to their mothers." And that was what had marred the day's perfection. The children Anne cared about the most, the ones who came to her nursery, couldn't enjoy Rob's magnificent merry-go-round. She laid a hand on his arm, as if that gesture would help him understand. "What I'm proposing is that you make a carousel with miniature horses. I want them small enough that my nursery children won't be frightened."

Again Rob shook his head. "It's a great idea, Anne, and I wish I could help you. The truth is, what's bothering me today isn't just the fact that this carousel is finished. It's also knowing that I can't stay in Hidden Falls any longer."

Anne didn't understand. Though she knew Rob envisioned himself as an itinerant carver, surely there was no reason he couldn't stay here long enough to build another carousel. "Why not? I'm certain Charles will let you continue to use the workshop."

"That's not the problem." Rob was silent for a long moment, and Anne could see the indecision on his face. He was weighing whatever he was going to say, trying to decide whether or not to trust her with it. At last he spoke. "I need to find my sister."

"Your sister?" Anne couldn't hide her surprise. Fearing that Rob would regret having said this much and would return to the converted stable, she took his hand and led him to the wrought iron bench. "I didn't know you had a sister," she said when they were seated. She wouldn't relinquish Rob's hand, lest he flee.

"I don't any more." His tone was bleak, telling her more clearly than his words how deeply he felt the loss. "When our parents died, no one in the family wanted to take two children, so I was sent to my father's brother and Edith went to my mother's sister. I haven't seen her since the day we both left the farm."

"Oh, Rob!" From the little he had said, Anne knew that life with his uncle hadn't been easy, but she hadn't guessed that the young boy had also suffered the loss of his only sibling. How awful! Anne couldn't imagine what her life would have been like if she and Jane and Charles had been separated.

"My uncle didn't have much use for girls, so he would never let me contact her." Anne tightened her grip on Rob's hand, trying to comfort him the only way she knew. "When I was old enough to leave the farm and make my own living, I started looking for Edith, only to discover that the aunt and uncle who had adopted her had left Philadelphia. No one knew where they'd gone. There was a lot of speculation, but they were all dead ends."

Anne nodded. Now she understood why Rob wrote so many letters. It wasn't that he was seeking more work. He was searching for his sister.

Rob turned so that he was facing Anne, his eyes filled with pain. "I don't know if you can understand this, but I feel as if part of me is missing. I need to know where Edith is and that she's happy. Until I do that, I can't think about my future. I can't settle down in Hidden Falls or anywhere until I find my sister."

Taking a deep breath, Anne tried to still the pounding of her heart. It had been horrible when her parents had died, but she had had Jane and Charles as well as the memory of many happy years. Rob had lost his entire family when he'd been a defenseless child. How dreadful!

Anne swallowed deeply, searching for the right words. What could she say, what could anyone say, when faced with such a tragedy? At length she settled for simple words, hoping he would understand how heartfelt they were. "I'm so sorry, Rob. I wish there were something I could do to help you."

For the first time that night, a crooked smile crossed Rob's face. "I wish that too. The truth is, it's going to take a miracle for me to find Edith, and right now miracles seem to be in short supply."

CHAPTER SEVEN

Rob was right. There were no miracles in sight. Anne had spent hours trying to think of ways to find Rob's sister, but all she had come up with were dead ends. The man didn't need any more of those. As for herself, while she wouldn't claim she needed a miracle, there was no doubt she needed something.

Though rain was not uncommon in late September, today was unseasonably cold and rainy. The children were restless, and nothing Anne did seemed to help. The older ones wanted Bertha to play with them; the younger ones were content if Bertha read them a story. Anne's role seemed to have been reduced to preparing their snack of milk and crackers.

She opened the small icebox and reached for a jug of milk, trying to bite back her disappointment. Compared to Rob's missing sister, this was trivial. Anne knew that just as she knew the way she was reacting was out of all proportion to the problem. She wasn't simply disappointed, she was jealous, and it was petty to be jealous. Anne knew that, and yet she couldn't change the way she felt. It hurt that the children preferred Bertha's company. The first time it had happened, Anne had thought it was a case of novelty, that the children were excited by having a new person care for them. But the novelty hadn't worn off. If anything, their attachment to Bertha had grown, relegating Anne to the background. They turned to her only if Bertha was not available.

Was it, she wondered, because of her scars? With the bluntness that seemed characteristic of children, one of the boys had asked her about them the first day he'd come to the nursery. Anne thought he and the other children had accepted her explanation, but perhaps she was wrong. Perhaps they were frightened by the ugliness.

Anne poured milk into the toddlers' cups, then started to warm some for the infants' bottles, all the while trying to keep a smile fixed on her face. The important thing was that the nursery was operational and that the children were happy there. Anne reminded herself of that again as she did at least a dozen times a day. She had accomplished her goal; she should be pleased. And she was. But there was no denying the fact that the youngsters' obvious preference for Bertha made Anne feel as if she were a failure. Again.

The year in Switzerland had given her time — perhaps too much time — to think. During that time she'd told herself that she could not undo the past. She couldn't change the fact that she had failed to save her parents, but she could be successful in the future. She could create a safe, happy place for the mill workers' youngest children, and at the same time she could fill the empty spot deep inside her. So far, she'd been only partially successful. The children were safe and happy, but the void inside Anne was larger than ever before.

"Are you all right?" The children were resting, one of the few times of the day when Anne and Bertha could also sit down. Today they had pulled their chairs into a corner and were talking quietly while they sipped coffee.

"I'm a bit out of sorts," Anne admitted, chagrined that her thoughts had been obvious. It wasn't Bertha's fault that the children preferred her. The problem was Anne, not her assistant. "It must be the rainy weather," she said, seizing on the first excuse she could find.

Bertha cradled her coffee cup between both hands and studied Anne's face. Something in her expression told Anne she hadn't believed her explanation. "I suppose that makes it worse," Bertha said at last. "I probably shouldn't have said anything at all." Bertha's face flushed with embarrassment. "My mother used to tell me that I needed to think before I spoke. I'm afraid I still haven't learned that lesson."

"It's all right, Bertha. I'm just sorry that my feelings were so obvious."

Bertha shook her head. "Most people wouldn't have noticed. The only reason I did is that I recognized the symptoms. Two years ago, I saw the same expression you've been wearing every time I looked in the mirror."

Anne tried not to let her distress show. This was more serious than she'd thought. How embarrassing that Bertha knew of her petty jealousy! She sipped her coffee, hoping to regain some semblance of composure.

"You may not be ready to admit it," Bertha continued. "I understand that, too. And I may be overstepping myself here. After all, you have a sister. I simply wanted to tell you that if you want to talk about it to another woman, I'm a good listener."

Anne took another sip of coffee to cover her confusion over the strange turn the conversation had just taken. If she wanted to admit to her jealousy, the last person Anne would choose as a confidante would be Bertha. How could she admit to this kind, generous woman that she envied her? "That's very gracious of you, Bertha," she said as firmly as she could, "but there's nothing wrong. It's simply the rain."

Raising both eyebrows, Bertha shook her head. "You can deny it, but you can't hide it."

A bad day had just turned worse, much worse. Anne's mortification was complete. "Oh, Bertha, I'm sorry. I never wanted you to know what I felt. I'm so ashamed." Anne knew she was babbling, but she couldn't help it.

"Ashamed?" Bertha leaned forward, the furrows between her eyes attesting to her surprise. "Why would you be ashamed of falling in love?"

Love? Bertha thought she was in love! What on earth had made her think that?

"You have two letters."

Rob had come to the post office as he did every day, hoping for a response to the dozens of inquiries he had sent, but not really expecting one. Today he had received two. Maybe the miracle he sought was inside one of them. Trying to camouflage his eagerness, Rob reached for the mail, feigning casualness as he looked at the postmarks. Little Valley! That had been the last lead he'd received. Surely this time there would be good news. Unable to wait any longer, Rob walked to the far corner of the post office and opened the envelope, his heart pounding with anticipation. This time would be different. It had to be.

As his eyes scanned the single sheet of paper, he tried not to frown. Another dead end. The mayor of Little Valley had made a series of inquiries, but there were no records of anyone resembling Edith ever having lived there. He regretted having to inform Rob, but . . . There was always a "but." This one was worse than the others, because Rob had no further leads. He'd exhausted every one, and still he hadn't found his sister.

Though Rob was tempted to crumple the envelope and hurl it across the room, he forced himself to slide it into his pocket, then glanced at the other. The postmark was New York. Rob stared at it for a moment, wondering who had written to him. He had sent no inquiries to New York, since the one thing everyone who had known his aunt and uncle had agreed on was that they had left Philadelphia for a smaller town. Knowing that, it seemed unlikely that Edith would be in a large city.

With a decided lack of enthusiasm, Rob opened the letter and perused its contents. As he did, his eyes widened in surprise. Though the letter brought him no closer to his sister, it could be the solution to one of his problems, if Anne was right. There was only one way to find out. Rob needed to talk to Charles.

"Is something wrong?" Charles asked when Rob appeared in his office at the mill a few minutes later. Though they had had many meetings to discuss the carousel, this was the first time Rob had been inside the mill.

He shook his head. "You have a nice office." The furniture was old-fashioned, probably dating from Charles's grandfather's era, but the room was spacious and boasted a large window. A tall plant filled one corner, while piles of papers threatened to topple over on the desk. Had it not been for the sound of looms thumping, this could have been the office of any prosperous businessman.

Charles settled back in his chair. "I don't

imagine you came here to critique the décor." Charles had never been one for pleasantries. Perhaps that was part of the secret of his success: he focused on the business at hand.

"Your assumption is accurate," Rob said. "I came to ask you for a favor." Quickly, Rob explained that the second letter he had received had been from a man in New York who wanted Rob to build a six-horse carousel for his children.

"That's good news, isn't it?"

"It is indeed." Rob's first reaction to the letter had been relief that he had more work for Mark and Luke. "The only problem is that my patron has no place for us to set up a workshop."

Charles had been tossing a paperweight from one hand to another. He laid it on the desk and leaned forward. "I don't see that as a problem. You've already got a workshop here. Keep using it. And when you're done, Brad's trains will transport the finished animals to New York."

That was what Anne had predicted Charles would say. "Are you sure it's not an imposition?" It had been one thing to work at Fairlawn when he was building a carousel for Charles. This was different. Although . . . Rob's thoughts began to whirl. There would be delays while he sketched the new horses and waited for the man in New York to approve the drawings. He could use that time to create the child-sized merry-go-round Anne wanted.

"Are you sure I'm not imposing?" he asked again. "You might have other plans for the building."

"Hardly! I can't envision ever again using it as a stable." Charles grinned. "The truth is, I've been thinking about buying a Model T. All I need to do is convince Susannah."

Rob wasn't surprised. Though there were only three automobiles in Hidden Falls, they were becoming common in the cities. "I've heard they're more trouble than a horse," he cautioned Charles.

"This is the twentieth century." Charles's grin said he had made his decision. "I think Henry Ford is right and that his horseless carriages will replace the animals. In a few years, the only horses left will be the ones you carve."

"Those don't go very far or very fast."

Charles shrugged. "That may be true, but they perform a more valuable function than mere transportation. Your horses have made my sister smile, and as far as I can see, that's close to a miracle."

If that was a miracle, Rob hoped he hadn't

exhausted the supply. He needed another one, and he needed it soon.

"Be careful, Fred." Though Anne reached for the small boy, she wasn't quick enough, and the accident that she had seen forming happened. Fred collided with the table, hitting his head on a corner.

"Ouch!" The boy's shock turned to tears when blood began to flow down his face. As the other children began to whimper, Anne exchanged looks with Bertha. Seconds later, her assistant had organized a story circle with the toddlers, leaving Anne alone with Fred.

"It'll be all right." Anne pulled the child onto her lap and wiped the blood away while she murmured words of comfort. Fortunately, the injury was not serious, though — as was characteristic of head wounds — it bled profusely. "You're a brave boy," she said as she staunched the bleeding and applied a bandage. "Now you look like the soldier in the book we were reading."

As Anne had hoped, Fred straightened his shoulders and rejoined the other children, announcing that he was a soldier. That problem had been resolved with relative ease. If only the others were as straightforward. Though she continued to wrack her brain, Anne was unable to find any avenues Rob had not explored in his search for Edith. She sighed. The only good thing that had happened in the last week was Rob's new carousel commission and the fact that it would keep him in Hidden Falls for a few more months. Perhaps by the time those horses were finished, Anne would have thought of a way to help Rob find his sister.

"I'm impressed," Bertha said as Anne closed the box of first aid supplies. "I doubt my father could have done any better."

Anne shrugged and placed the box on the top shelf where curious children could not reach it. "I've spent a lot of time with doctors and nurses over the past year. It's only to be expected that I would learn a few things from them."

She walked to the window, watching drops of rain slide down the glass, remembering all the physicians she had consulted, beginning with Bertha's father and ending with the doctor in Switzerland. In between, there had been a seemingly endless number of physicians in New York City.

The rain reminded Anne of Dr. Muller. It had been a rainy day when she had first met him, the last of the New York physicians on Charles's list. Because he was a young doctor with less experience than the others, Charles had doubted he could help Anne, but there was no one else left to consult. Her brother had been partially right. Though she had spent a month in Dr. Muller's care, he had finally announced that he could not help her. He had, however, provided what proved to be invaluable help by recommending a doctor in Switzerland. "I'll have Delia give you his address, and I'll prepare a letter of reference for him," Dr. Muller had said at Anne's last appointment. Delia, the nurse who had tried so valiantly to help Anne, didn't bother trying to hide the tears in her eyes as she handed Anne the piece of paper. She'd been. . . .

The memory hit Anne with the force of one of Brad's locomotives, and she gripped the windowsill, trying to keep her legs from buckling. Delia's eyes! No wonder Rob had seemed so familiar when she had first met him. In the past few weeks Anne hadn't thought about Rob's eyes. As she'd grown to know him, she had stopped focusing on any one feature. But now as memories assailed her from all directions, she remembered how the familiarity had teased the corners of her consciousness. The reason was now clear. Rob had Delia's eyes.

Anne took a deep breath, exhaling slowly.

Could it be? Could Delia be Rob's Edith? Though the names were different, there was a definite physical resemblance between Rob and Delia. Anne thought rapidly, trying to remember everything the young nurse had told her. Hadn't she mentioned that she had no family in New York and that she was living with other nurses in a small apartment? That could mean that her foster parents had died, leaving her on her own.

Anne stared out the window, scarcely seeing the rain as she considered her course of action. Rob had chased so many dead ends that she hesitated to tell him of her suspicions, lest they be unfounded. It would be cruel to raise his hopes if the woman wasn't his sister. Anne wouldn't tell Rob about Delia until she had done a bit of investigating on her own. She would write to Dr. Muller today, asking for information about his nurse. And if Delia was Rob's sister? Anne smiled. It might not be a miracle, but it would be close enough for her.

"I don't want to go to this party." Jane had brought her gown into Anne's room, and as they had so many times in the past, the sisters were helping each other dress.

Anne wasn't much more enthusiastic than her twin. Ever since she had sent the letter to New York, she had been able to think of little else than when she would receive Dr. Muller's response. Though she had hoped that some of Charles's former colleagues and one or two members of the Mythological Society could have been invited to this party, Charles had refused, insisting that tonight remain a celebration of her and Jane's return. When he had seen Anne's disappointment, her brother had promised that he and Susannah would host a weekend of events for potential carousel customers in November. But that was six weeks away. There was still tonight and the ordeal of being the center of attention as people saw how different the once identical Moreland twins had become.

"You know we have no choice." Anne tried to keep her voice neutral. "The party's in our honor."

She looked at the two ball gowns draped across the bed. In the past she and Jane had chosen the same style gown but in different colors. Tonight they were both wearing blue. Tonight there was no question of anyone confusing them. Jane's gown reflected the latest fashion, its artfully draped bodice revealing her creamy smooth neck, while Anne's featured a high laced-trimmed collar designed expressly to hide her no longer smooth skin. Though the style was more suited to an aging matron than a young woman, it was preferable to having people repulsed by her scars.

Jane fastened her stockings, then reached for the first petticoat. "Tonight wouldn't be so awful if Matt were going."

As Anne slid her feet into her dancing slippers, she looked up at her sister. This was the first time she had heard that Matt would not attend the party. "Why isn't he coming? I know he received an invitation."

Jane gave out an exasperated sigh. "He said it wouldn't be proper. He said," she emphasized the words, making it clear that she did not share Matt's opinion, "that if he's supposed to be an advocate for the workers, he shouldn't be socializing with the robber barons."

Anne picked up her sister's gown, ready to help her as she'd done so many times before. "Charles and the Harrods aren't robbing anyone."

"That's not the way some people see it." Jane's voice was muffled as she slid the dress over her head. "Leave it to me to get involved with a man who has principles!"

Anne nodded slowly as she began to fasten the back of Jane's gown. "You love him, don't you?"

Though Anne couldn't see her sister's face, she could hear the annoyance in her voice. "I'm not going to admit that any more than you'll admit you love Rob."

Anne's fingers faltered, and she found herself unable to thread the loop over the last button. *Love Rob? Where had Jane gotten that crazy idea? Had she been talking to Bertha Kellogg?* "I don't love him," she announced.

Jane whirled around to face her sister. "See what I mean? I knew you wouldn't admit it." She looked down at her gown, then reached for Anne's. "We'd better get you dressed. They can't start the party without the guests of honor."

Mrs. Harrod had outdone herself. The ballroom was filled with fresh flowers, their fragrances blending with the women's perfumes. A string quartet occupied one corner, their soft melodies providing a counterpoint to the guests' voices. And in an adjoining room, a table laden with silver platters promised a delicious ending to the evening. Rose Walk had never looked more beautiful. It could have been a scene out of a fairytale except. . . . Anne took a deep breath. She would be all right if she didn't look that way.

She smiled at Brad's mother. "Everything

164

is perfect," she lied, refusing to spoil the woman's pleasure. Her hostess returned the smile, then nodded at her husband.

"Ladies and gentlemen, if I might have your attention." Mr. Harrod led Anne and Jane to the center of the ballroom. "As you know, this evening is in honor of two of Hidden Falls' most beautiful women. Let us all welcome Anne and Jane Moreland back to our town."

When the applause subsided, the string quartet played the first notes of a waltz. "I have only one problem," Mr. Harrod said with a rueful grin. "How can I lead the first dance when we have two guests of honor?"

As if on cue, Brad walked to his father's side. He looked at Jane, then seeing the almost imperceptible shaking of her head, offered his arm to Anne.

"It's hopeless, isn't it?" he asked as they whirled around the dance floor, now crowded with other guests.

Anne pretended not to know what Brad meant. "What seems hopeless?"

"Loving Jane."

She hadn't been mistaken. The man who had been their childhood playmate had what Anne's mother would have called tender sentiments for Jane. Anne had suspected that, just as she suspected Jane was well aware of Brad's feelings. "I honestly don't know," she told Brad. "At one time I thought I knew almost everything Jane was thinking, but now . . . now it's different." Though Jane appeared to be in love with Matt Wagner, that might be only infatuation.

Brad nodded, then asked Anne about her nursery in a deliberate attempt to change the subject.

"May I interrupt?" His father tapped Brad's shoulder, indicating that they should change partners. As she whirled around the room in Mr. Harrod's arms, Anne looked at her sister. Though she had refused Brad initially, now Jane was smiling as if she had not a care in the world, as if Brad were the perfect partner. Was it true, or was she simply acting a part? Anne wished she knew. Just as she wished she knew where Rob was. He had said he would attend the party, but Anne had not seen him.

As she had expected, neither Anne nor Jane was without a partner for a single dance. Almost every man who had been invited appeared to believe it was his duty to dance with both of them. Even Rob, who had finally made a belated appearance, had offered his arm to Jane, though he had not yet approached Anne. She wouldn't think about that. She wouldn't wonder why any more than she would look at the flickering candles in the chandelier. She would focus on her partner and the intricate dance steps. And when this number ended, she would speak to the only guests who remained on the sidelines, apparently unwilling to dance: her father's former advisors, Ralph and Philip.

"Would you be willing to dance with an old man?" As if her thoughts had conjured him, Ralph appeared at Anne's side when the last note faded and her partner made his final bow.

She smiled and nodded at the portly attorney who had provided her with wise counsel as well as friendship. "Only if you stop referring to yourself that way." She moved into his arms, thankful that the song was a slow one. But, despite her concerns, Ralph danced with an ease that belied his age and girth, and Anne found herself relaxing for the first time since she had arrived at the party.

"You need to stop monopolizing our guest of honor." The other man who had sat out all the earlier dances tapped Ralph's shoulder with more force than necessary.

Anne blinked, surprised by both the fact that Philip was on the dance floor and that he was cutting in on Ralph rather than wait for the next song. Ralph appeared equally surprised. Though he released Anne, a flush colored the lawyer's face. "I would hardly call one dance a monopoly."

"One is more than you deserve." Philip's voice seethed with hostility, reminding Anne of the times he had advised her not to trust Ralph. Was this more of their lifelong rivalry, or was there another cause? In either case, the Harrods' party was neither the time nor the place to air grievances.

"I don't know why you're complaining." At least Ralph kept his voice low, only his stiff posture betraying his anger. "It's not as if you planned to dance with either Anne or Jane. Everyone knows you haven't danced since Rosemary died." At first, the townspeople had thought it was simply that Philip was in extended mourning, but then, as the years had passed, speculation had risen that he had made a promise to his wife never to dance again.

"There's always a first time." Bowing slightly, Philip turned to Anne. "May I have the honor of this dance?"

Thankful that she could stop the arguing by the simple expedient of separating the men, Anne moved into Philip's arms, giving Ralph a warm smile of farewell.

Philip tightened his grip on her, holding her closer than convention dictated as he guided her toward the edge of the dance floor. "Oh, Mary, you have no idea how long I've waited for this."

Mary! Anne was so startled that she missed a step. "I'm not Mary." She struggled to control the pounding of her heart. *Why had Philip called her by her mother's name?* "I'm Anne."

Philip looked down at her, his blue eyes clouded. "Of course you are Anne. That's what I said."

It wasn't. Anne would say no more, for it must have been a slip of the tongue. She told herself there was no reason to be concerned about the older man's confusion. Hadn't she heard that sometimes happened with age? Still, she was grateful when the dance ended.

"I feel almost guilty asking you for a dance," Rob said an hour later as he extended his arm to Anne. It was the first time he'd spoken to her all evening, though their eyes had met across the dance floor more times than Anne could count. Now that he was here, the empty feeling that she had been unable to dispel, watching Rob dance with other women and wishing she were his partner, was gone.

"Guilty? Why?" As Rob placed his hand on the back of her waist, Anne felt a shiver of delight course through her veins.

"There are still men waiting for a turn with you, but you and I have already danced."

Anne chuckled, remembering. "This time is different. This time we have a wooden floor and musicians."

"And dozens of other people."

She thought of the afternoon they had danced on the grass behind the nursery. "You're right," she agreed. "That was special." But so was being held in his arms again. If Anne had her way, this song would never end.

The dance steps took them to the edge of the floor. As they reached it, someone opened one of the French doors. Though the breeze was welcome in a room that was becoming overheated by all the dancing, it set the candles in the wall sconces to flickering. Anne stared, mesmerized, then shuddered as the flames appeared to touch the wall.

"What's wrong?"

She felt the blood draining from her face and gripped Rob's arm to steady herself. "The candles," she said, gesturing toward the wall. The breeze had subsided, and the candles had stopped flickering. There was no longer any danger. There probably had never been any. "It's silly of me to worry so much. I know that I need to overcome my fears." Anne took a deep breath and forced herself to look at the candles again. When she turned back to Rob, she said softly, "I wish I weren't so weak."

Under the guise of the dance steps, he led her away from the open flames. "You're wrong, Anne." Though his voice was low, ensuring that they would not be overheard, there was no denying its intensity. "You're not weak. You're the strongest person I've ever met." Rob looked down at her, his blue eyes shining with an emotion Anne could not identify. "I can't tell you how much I admire that."

She nodded slowly. Rob's words were kind and genuine. It was only Anne who longed for more, but, oh how she wished that what Rob felt for her was more than admiration.

CHAPTER EIGHT

Anne frowned as she looked at her notes. Rob might be the most talented carousel carver in the country — and she was convinced he was — but one thing he was not was a shrewd businessman. She frowned again, thinking of the conversation they'd had about what Anne called the commercial aspects of his work. Rob's lack of interest could not have been more obvious. When she had asked him how he priced his horses, he had shrugged. "Whatever it costs me plus a little." That, Anne knew, was not a recipe for success.

She stared at the pile of bills he'd given her and shook her head in dismay. The man's filing system was a disaster! And yet as she looked at the disorganized mess, Anne couldn't help smiling. Rob might not know how to set up a proper accounting system any more than he knew how to market his talent, but she knew someone who did. Her father had seen to it that all of his children understood the fundamentals of business. Charles had excelled at finding ways to make production more efficient; Jane seemed to have an instinctive knowledge of which finished products would be the best sellers; while Anne alone enjoyed the paperwork. She had felt as if she had won a treasure hunt the day she had discovered a way to increase the mill's profitability by a penny a yard. If she could do that with a well run operation like Moreland Mills, surely she would be able to help Rob.

She was so engrossed in creating income and expense charts that the knock on the front door barely registered. When it was repeated, Anne laid down her pen and rose. There was no one else to answer the door.

"Good afternoon, Philip." Her smile owed more to the fact that she had remembered the correct appellation than pleasure that he'd come to call. Though it still seemed strange not to call him "Uncle Philip," she had managed it.

The tall, thin man who stood on the front porch, one arm behind his back, did not return her smile. Instead, his face wore an expression Anne had never seen. Philip appeared serious, but there was something more, something Anne could not identify, in the look that he gave her. Was something wrong? Was that the reason Philip had come here today, when he had seen her only last night at the party?

"Come in," Anne invited as she tried not to let her imagination conjure scenes of disaster. In all likelihood, despite Philip's odd expression, this was nothing more than a friendly call.

Philip shook his head and remained on the porch. "Thank you, my dear, but there's no need for that. I came for two reasons." The first was evident when he extended the arm that had been hidden behind his back. "I hope you'll accept this small token of my esteem."

There was nothing small about the bouquet of red roses that he handed her. It was enormous. The flowers were also out of season, which meant that Philip had gone to considerable trouble and expense to acquire them. Why? Anne bent her head and sniffed the roses to cover her confusion. No one had ever brought her such an extravagant gift. Philip was a family friend. He and Rosemary had given all the Moreland children gifts for their birthdays and Christmas, but it still felt strange to accept the flowers. They were much more than a small token.

Before Anne could murmur her thanks, Philip continued, "The second reason I came was that I thought perhaps you would like to take a drive." He gestured toward his automobile. "It's a lovely day for a ride in the country."

Anne could not deny that, just as she could not deny her reluctance. She sniffed the flowers again as she tried to formulate a response. What she wanted was to stay home and work on Rob's business plans. She did not want to go for a drive in the country unless it was with . . . Anne clenched her fists. There was no point in thinking of things that would never happen. She looked from the roses to Philip's Model T, remembering how her mother had impressed on her children the need to be polite. It would be rude to refuse Philip's request.

"A short ride would be pleasant," Anne said at last. Philip smiled, then helped her into the Model T, cranked the starter and climbed into the driver's seat.

"The roses are beautiful," Anne said as they drove slowly through Hidden Falls. Because it was Sunday afternoon, the one day the mill was closed, the streets were filled with families enjoying the sunshine. They looked up in curiosity as the automobile passed, and Anne knew that the story of her and Philip's ride would be repeated a hundred times before the sun set.

Rather than dwell on the rumor mill's possible speculation, Anne sought a neutral topic. "Our garden has suffered dreadfully from neglect." Though the formal garden had been her mother's pride, no one had touched it since her death. "Perhaps Jane or I will have time to work there next year."

Philip turned onto a country lane. The maple trees were changing to their autumn orange, while the oaks had already turned to gold. It was Anne's favorite time of the year. As beautiful as Switzerland was, she had missed her home's fall finery.

Her sigh of pleasure was interrupted as Philip slowed the Model T and turned toward her. "Perhaps next year you'll be in your own home with a garden of your own."

This time Anne did sigh, for Philip's words conjured the image of a small plot with hollyhocks standing sentinel in the back, while masses of white and purple alyssum perfumed the air. In her mind, Anne saw herself kneeling in front of the flowerbed, pulling weeds, while Rob tilled the ground for an herb garden. Though the house was indistinct, Anne knew a white picket fence enclosed the yard. And within that yard a young boy with Rob's eyes and her own sandy blond hair tossed a ball to his puppy. Anne closed her eyes in a desperate attempt to keep the image from fading.

"That's a lovely dream," she said softly, "but I'm afraid that's all it is. A dream."

Philip reached across the seat and laid his hand on hers. "Sometimes dreams come true."

If only she could believe that!

The evening was warmer than normal, almost summerlike with a light breeze carrying the scent of grass and the air filled with the chirp of crickets. Anne half expected to see fireflies as soon as the sun set, but the fireflies, she knew, had left for the season. This evening she and Rob were seated on the brick patio behind Fairlawn, a pitcher of lemonade on the table between them.

"I organized your bills," she told Rob. What she wouldn't tell him was that she thought it a minor miracle that he wasn't being dunned by creditors. How he found anything in the satchel he'd been using for a filing system was a mystery to her.

"And?" Rob had seemed pleased and a bit relieved when Anne had suggested she help him price the new carousel. It was, she had insisted, the least she could do since he had agreed to make the miniature merry-go-round for her nursery children. Besides, although it was something she wouldn't tell him, organizing Rob's paperwork helped keep her from counting the days since she had posted the letter to Dr. Muller.

Anne refilled Rob's glass. "I imagine Charles would be happy to know that you gave him a real bargain. The truth is, Rob, you charged him far too little." When Rob started to shake his head, Anne continued. "I've done some research on other companies' prices, and their horses sold for substantially more than yours, even though they weren't as ornate and didn't use such expensive materials." She had been shocked by the cost of the lead horse's gold leaf mane and the jewels that decorated all of the animals.

Rob shook his head, obviously disagreeing. "Your brother took a chance on me. He deserved a fair price for that."

Charles had gotten far more than a fair price. He'd paid only a fraction of the carousel's worth. "I'm not suggesting we ask Charles for more money. It's too late for that, but we can use the Hidden Falls carousel in our advertising."

"Advertising?" The look Rob gave her told

Anne he had not considered that aspect of business. She wasn't surprised.

"How else will people learn about the wonderful horses you create if we don't tell them?" Anne had started getting prices for advertisements in the major newspapers. Initially they would focus on the East Coast. Then, once Ludlow Carousels was well established, they could expand to other parts of the country.

Rob stretched his legs in front of him, crossing them at the ankles as he leaned back. To the casual observer, he appeared to be the picture of relaxation, but Anne saw the faint tightening of his fingers on the chair arm as he asked, "How much do you think I should charge for the new carousel?"

She told him.

All pretense of relaxation disappeared. Rob sat up straight and stared at her. "That much?"

Anne took a sip of lemonade to hide her smile. She had known he'd react that way. The man had no sense of his own value. "That's only an introductory rate," she said as she placed her glass back on the table. "Once you've built three or four carousels and your name is well known, we'll charge more."

Rob continued to stare at her, almost as if

she were an unfamiliar species of animal in the zoo. "Where did you learn all that?"

"From my father." She told him about the lessons her father had given all his children. "Admittedly, carousel horses are different products from fine cottons, but the concepts are the same."

Rob was still shaking his head, as if in wonder, when two small dogs launched themselves at him, putting muddy paws on his knees.

"Down, Salt! Come here, Pepper." Susannah called to the dogs at the same time that Charles asked if he and Susannah were interrupting a private discussion. Anne shook her head.

"Your sister was explaining that I undercharged you for the carousel," Rob said with a wry smile. "Drastically undercharged."

"Are you trying to bankrupt me, sister dear?" Charles asked in mock severity as he found a chair for his wife, then settled himself on another.

Anne shook her head again. "All I'm trying to do is help Rob earn what he's worth." And it was the most exhilarating thing she had ever done. Even running the nursery didn't give her the same sense of satisfaction that helping Rob did. For the first time in her life, Anne felt as if she was accomplishing something that only she could do, and, oh, what a glorious feeling that was. Bertha might be better with the children, but Anne knew that no one else in Hidden Falls could have done a better job creating a business plan for Rob. Her life would be complete if only Dr. Muller would answer her letter.

"Mr. Biddle is here again." Though the words were noncommittal, Mrs. Enke's voice telegraphed her disapproval.

Anne looked up from the towels she was folding. Since laundry for the nursery more than doubled Mrs. Enke's work, Anne had volunteered to help with it. She and Jane were both concerned that Mrs. Enke, who refused to let them hire an assistant for her, would soon announce her retirement. That thought was far more disagreeable than Philip's continued visits.

"Please tell him I'll be with him in a minute." Anne straightened her skirt, then checked her appearance in the mirror, all the while wondering why Philip had come. This was the third time in a week.

"My dear, you look more beautiful than ever." He stood in the parlor, as perfectly groomed as ever. Anne doubted the man ever had a hair out of place, while Rob . . .

She bit the inside of her cheek. It was foolish to entertain thoughts of Rob.

"I hope you'll accept this small token of my esteem." Philip's words were the same that he used each time. Only the gift varied. This time he proffered a large box of candy.

"That's very generous of you, Philip, but there's no need to bring me a gift when you come to visit." First the flowers, then an obviously expensive leatherbound book, now this.

He smiled and took her hand in his. "There's a difference between needing to do something and wanting to do it. I wanted," he emphasized the word, "to bring you these trifles."

They weren't trifles. Though the gifts of candy, books, and flowers were ones her mother would have approved, the extravagance would have made Mrs. Moreland's eyebrows rise. Anne looked at the man who was holding her hand so tightly. What could she say?

"Thank you."

"I heard Uncle Philip was here again." Jane settled into the chair on the opposite side of the desk where Anne was calculating potential profits on Rob's new carousel. "What did he bring you this time?"

"Candy." Anne gestured toward the still unopened box. Though she liked candy and knew that this chocolatier was considered the finest in the state, Anne felt an inexplicable reluctance to eat even a single piece. "Would you like some, Jane? If not, I thought I'd take it to the nursery tomorrow." As her sister raised an eyebrow, Anne continued, "The children deserve a treat."

The look Jane gave the confectionary box told Anne she also had no intention of sampling the contents. "Uncle Philip won't be happy if he hears that you've given his candy away."

"Why not?"

Jane's laugh was short and brittle. "Oh, Anne. Open your eyes. The man is courting you."

Anne's eyes opened, not in recognition but in shock. "That's preposterous!"

The man was courting her. Any fool could see that. Rob finished spreading glue on the pieces of wood, then reached for the clamp. He couldn't blame Philip. Anne was a beautiful woman with so much to offer. Of course Philip would be attracted to her. But Anne? Surely she could do better than Philip Biddle.

Rob clamped the wood together and laid

it aside. These two pieces would form part of one leg. Though he had hoped to carve tonight, thoughts of Anne and Philip were whirling through his mind with such force that he didn't trust his hands to hold a gouge steady. Instead, he decided to start assembling the pieces of basswood for the next horse. While he waited for his patron in New York to select the six designs he preferred from the dozen Rob had sent him, Rob and his assistants had begun work on the small carousel for Anne's nursery. Together he and Anne had decided that they would have four pair of horses and two chariots, reasoning that the infants could be carried onto the chariot so that all of Anne's children could ride at once.

Children! That was another reason Anne shouldn't marry Philip. For Pete's sake, the man was old enough to be her father. Rob ran his hand down the side of the wood, verifying that it was smooth. He should concentrate on his carving, but he couldn't, not when he was worried about Anne. She deserved someone better than Philip. She deserved someone her own age who could give her a home, children, and a long life together, not simply bunches of out-of-season roses and expensive books.

Rob opened the glue and began to brush

it on the wood. The basswood was perfect; the horse would be a good one. Rob knew that instinctively, just as he knew that he would never be able to give Anne all she deserved. Even if he charged the exorbitant rates she had suggested for his carousels, it would be many, many years — if ever — before he could afford to buy her fancy ball gowns or build her a house like Fairlawn. And, even if she didn't mind living in a tiny house and walking through town rather than being driven in an automobile, there was no ignoring the fact that Anne was an educated woman, part of society, while he was nothing more than a glorified carpenter.

And if that weren't enough, he needed to find Edith before he could even think about settling down. He needed to know that Aunt Agnes hadn't mistreated Edith, or — if she had — he needed to find a way to help his sister forget. Rob shuddered, thinking of the pinches and slaps he had endured during a short visit. Surely Aunt Agnes hadn't been so cruel to Edith.

Rob frowned as he clamped the second leg together. No matter how you looked at it, one thing was perfectly evident. He and Anne had no future together. None at all. And, knowing that, a wise man would stop torturing himself with dreams that would never come true.

Rob was not a wise man, he realized when he smelled Anne's perfume an instant before he heard the soft knock on the door. Though he knew it was all wrong, he couldn't help smiling at the thought of spending time with Anne.

"Didn't you tell me that you shouldn't be working this late because the light isn't good enough?"

When Rob merely shrugged rather than admit that he had come to the workshop hoping that the effort of carving would keep him from picturing Anne and Philip together, she walked to the horse he had been carving earlier that day. It was destined to be the lead horse on the small merry-go-round. Pointing toward the legs that were bent backwards, she asked, "Won't there be any feet on the ground?"

Rob shook his head. Though he and Anne had initially considered making the nursery carousel a miniature version of the original one, they had quickly discarded that idea, preferring that the two merry-go-rounds be different. "I thought I'd make all of the horses on this one jumpers, even though I prefer the look of the prancers. Those are the ones with their hind legs on the ground," he said, not sure that he had ever explained the difference between standers, with all four feet on the ground, prancers, and jumpers. "To me, prancers are more elegant than these jumpers, but children will probably like the fact that jumpers go up and down." For the Hidden Falls carousel, Rob had used prancers in the front row, adding jumpers when Charles had asked him to expand the merry-go-round with an inner row of animals.

Anne ran her fingers along the mane of the horse that had caught her attention. "This is wonderful," she said, smiling with obvious pleasure. "It looks like her mane is blowing in the wind. Let's call her Lillian." It had been Anne's suggestion that they name each of the horses for the small merry-go-round. She touched Lillian again. "I think this will be my favorite."

"Better than the lead horse on your carousel?"

Anne appeared shocked. "Oh, no. Nothing will ever compare to that. I meant my favorite of this carousel. I can picture each of the children riding on it."

She walked toward the wall where Rob had hung the sketches of the horses he had proposed for the New York merry-go-round. Though her voice was steady, something in the way she moved made Rob think that

Anne was nervous. It was surely only his imagination. But when she spoke, there was the slightest of tremors in her voice. What could be troubling Anne? Rob gritted his teeth, hoping it wasn't something Philip Biddle had done or said. Rob chided himself. Just because he didn't like Philip didn't mean the man was a scoundrel. Still, something was troubling Anne.

"I haven't been to the falls since I returned," she said, the trembling in her voice more prominent now. "I thought I might go there this evening." Anne hesitated, and this time Rob saw her fingers clench. "Can I persuade you to accompany me?"

Rob blinked in surprise. Could Anne be nervous about inviting him to walk with her? Surely not. Still, it was the first time she had asked him to do something for her. In the past, many of Anne's requests had been for the children. Even when she had encouraged him to attend the Harrods' party, she had couched her persuasion in terms of his career, telling him it was important that he learn to be at ease in social situations. This was different. Even though it was only a small request, it was one that Anne was making for herself. Rob suspected that she was not accustomed to having others consider her welfare. All except for Philip Biddle. The man had taken her riding, and Rob had seen him approaching the house, bearing very large gifts.

Rob thrust away thoughts of that old man and Anne. She hadn't invited Philip Biddle to walk to the falls with her. For Pete's sake, the man was so ancient he probably couldn't walk that far. Anne had asked him, and that thought made his pulse accelerate.

He shouldn't go. Rob knew that. He shouldn't spend any more time with her. They had no future, and each day that they spent together would make leaving more difficult. Rob knew that, too. He wouldn't go. He opened his mouth to refuse, but the words that came out were not the ones he intended. "I can't think of anything I would enjoy more." Rob crooked his arm and placed Anne's hand on it.

It was the perfect evening for a walk. The air was cool and crisp, reminding him that fall had arrived. The sky was a deep blue, now tinged with the roses and oranges of the approaching sunset. A few birds chirped as he and Anne strolled along River Road. It was a scene of idyllic splendor, yet Rob was only dimly aware of it, for all his senses were focused on the woman at his side, the woman whose hand sent waves of warmth through his arm, the woman whose light perfume teased his nostrils, the woman whose sweet voice sounded more melodic than any songbird.

They talked as they walked, but afterwards, Rob could not remember a single thing they had said. All he knew was that there was something wonderful, something almost magical, about spending this evening with Anne.

When they turned onto the steep path leading to the falls, he reached for the hand that was nestled in the bend of his elbow and clasped it in his, lest this precious woman slip and fall. And even when the danger was past and they were once more on level ground, he kept her hand in his.

Moments later they reached the first spot where the falls were visible. The roar of the rushing water was louder here as it cascaded over the rocky cliff, sending up a fine mist as it crashed onto the boulders at its base. Rob took a deep breath, trying to slow the pounding of his heart. The cataract was beautiful at any time of the day, but as the setting sun cast its golden glow, Rob was certain he had never seen anything so magnificent. Yet it wasn't the spectacular falls that caused his heart to beat more loudly than a snare drum. It was the woman who stood at his side.

"This is so beautiful." Anne whispered the words, as if afraid to destroy the magic of the moment by speaking too loudly. The hesitation that he had heard in the workshop was gone, and she was once more the woman who had a starring role in his dreams each night, the woman who seemed unaware of just how beautiful she was.

"So are you."

Her eyes widened slightly, and Rob saw the doubt in them. How could she not realize how special she was? Didn't she know how often he dreamed of her and how he longed to kiss her? He shouldn't. Rob knew that. But even as he told himself how foolish it would be, he drew her into his arms and lowered his lips to hers.

They had kissed before, and that wonderful moment had fueled his dreams. Rob had thought nothing could be better. He was wrong. Nothing could compare to this. As his pulse began to race and every sense was heightened, Rob knew that there had never been a kiss like this. Nothing had ever felt so right. Anne fit into his arms as if she were made for him; her soft sigh stirred him more than the most famous of symphonies; and surely there was nothing on earth as sweet as her lips. He pulled her tighter. If only this moment could last forever!

CHAPTER NINE

It was silly of her. Anne pulled out a large platter and began to arrange Mrs. Enke's freshly baked muffins on it. The children would start arriving in a few minutes, and though they should all have eaten breakfast at home, Anne knew that some did not. When she had heard several stomachs rumbling well before the mid-morning snack time, she had started bringing additional food. That wasn't silly. What was silly was the way Anne had acted last night. If Jane knew, she would have laughed, telling Anne she was behaving like a schoolgirl.

She should have been sleeping. That was what a wise person would have done. Instead, Anne had tossed and turned, reliving those wonderful moments in Rob's arms.

Each time she closed her eyes, she could picture his lips curving upward as he smiled at her. She could smell the faintly astringent combination of wood, paint, and hair tonic that clung to him. She could hear the catch in his breath the moment before his lips met hers. Most of all, she could feel the warmth of his lips on hers, the light prickle of an errant whisker, the strength of his arms around her body. The memories circled through her mind like the horses on one of Rob's carousels, revolving to a song she could not hear but one she hoped would have no end.

Though the kiss had been over all too soon, the memories did not cease. At length, when she had realized that slumber would continue to elude her, Anne had risen and, dragging a chair next to the window, had stared outside, the tenor of her thoughts changing. How could she have been so forward as to ask Rob to walk with her? If she were still alive, Mama would have been shocked. A lady didn't behave in such a fashion. A lady waited for the gentleman to suggest an outing. But Anne hadn't waited. Why hadn't she?

She could blame it on her confusion. There was no doubt that Jane's words had raised a host of questions, questions Anne wasn't certain she wanted to answer. Was Philip truly courting her? Jane would undoubtedly call her naïve, but until her sister had presented her interpretation of his intentions, Anne had told herself that he was visiting her as he would any family friend. Philip was lonely. That was why he had come so often. When the past few weeks were viewed through Jane's eyes, Anne had to admit that she had been deluding herself. Philip's gifts were part of the courting tradition, and the way he often held her hand longer than mere courtesy demanded added credence to Jane's assertion. So too did the fact that Anne was the only woman with whom Philip had danced at the Harrods' party.

Anne drew a pitcher of milk from the icebox and placed it next to the muffins. Bertha would be here in a few minutes, followed closely by the children.

Philip's courting — and it was difficult to deny that that was what he was doing — raised another, far more troubling, question. How did that make Anne feel? Perhaps she hadn't been truthful the day that Susannah had asked her about her dreams. Anne had dreams, the same ones many women cherished. From early childhood on, she had dreamt of love and marriage and children. It was simply that the last year had made her put those dreams aside, believing that no man would want to marry her. Now it appeared that one man might.

Anne opened the top half of the Dutch door, then closed it again. The October morning was still too cool to let in the fresh air, but — oh! — how she needed fresh air to clear the cobwebs from her mind. Though she had dreamed of marriage, never once had Anne pictured Philip as her groom. And yet, she couldn't deny that marriage to Philip would offer many things. She would live in comfort with a man who cared for her. She would never have to leave Hidden Falls and face strangers who were repulsed by her scars. Her brother could cease his worrying, for she would be settled.

Anne's head told her that, if Philip proposed marriage, she should accept his offer. It was the prudent thing to do. But her heart? Her heart told her something far different. Her heart still dreamed of love, of marriage to a man who made her pulse race and her heart sing, a man like Rob. That was why Anne had gone to the workshop last night, to talk to that man, to see whether her heart was wrong.

And then he had kissed her, and all thoughts of practical, prudent decisions had been driven from her mind. That was why she had spent the night remembering how wonderful it had felt to be held in his arms, how sweet his lips had been, and how she had wished the kiss would never end. Anne couldn't deny it. She loved Rob, and his kiss had made her think that maybe — just maybe — he loved her too.

Morning's light had brought a dose of reality. With the first rays of sun came the realization that Rob cared for her. Perhaps he even loved her a little, but if he did, it was only as a friend. A man like Rob Ludlow couldn't love a woman like Anne enough to marry her. What he felt for her was friendship, sympathy, and — perhaps — a bit of pity. After all, what else would a man who created such beauty feel for a woman whose beauty had been destroyed?

Anne gripped a chair back, trying to control her emotions. Bertha and the children would be here soon. She couldn't burden them with her sadness. It was bad enough that she'd imposed on Rob's kindness last night. Anne took a deep breath and exhaled slowly. There was no point in railing at her fate. The fire had changed her, both inside and out, and there was no undoing those changes. She had to live with them, just as she needed to be grateful for what she had been given and not long for anything more. For longing would bring nothing but heartache.

Rob had given her friendship. It was a

wonderful gift, and even if it wasn't everything she sought, it was all he had to offer. There was no point in dreaming dreams that would never come true. Instead, Anne would be the best friend Rob could ever want. She would help him make Ludlow Carousels a success. Perhaps she could even help him achieve his heart's desire.

Looking at the calendar, Anne counted the days since she had mailed the letter to Dr. Muller. By now he should have responded. During the months he had treated her, Anne had learned the doctor's routine. She knew that he rarely took holidays, and even when he attended meetings with other physicians, he scheduled them so that he was gone from the office no more than one week. Knowing that, Anne didn't understand why she hadn't received an answer, unless . . .

She heard the sound of children approaching, one admonishing the other not to lose her handkerchief. It wasn't only handkerchiefs that could be lost. Letters could too. That must be what had happened. Anne nodded as she heard Bertha greeting the children. The day was about to begin. She could do nothing now, but when it ended, Anne would write another letter to the doctor.

Normally the days passed quickly. Today was an exception. Today the ten hours felt as long as ten days, with Anne looking at the clock so many times that even one of the children commented on her preoccupation. It wasn't simply that she was anxious to send the doctor a second inquiry. That was important, but even more importantly, this would be the first time she had seen Rob since their kiss. Would he mention it? Would he try to kiss her again? And if he did, how would she react? Anne couldn't stop her heart from racing at the thought of being with Rob again. She looked at the clock for the hundredth time. Had it stopped?

At last the school day ended. The children scampered home. Where was Rob? Bertha had already left, and still there was no sign of Rob. Anne stood in front of the nursery, wondering what had delayed him. Normally he was as punctual as the mill workers, arriving at exactly the same time each day. But today was different. Today he wasn't here. Although Anne told herself there might be dozens of reasons why he was late, she could think of only one: Rob didn't want to see her. He regretted the kiss and was reluctant to face her again.

Anne opened her watch. Ten minutes. Rob

was ten minutes late. Perhaps he wasn't coming at all. As her heart plummeted at the thought, she saw him turn from Bridge onto Mill. Relieved, Anne began to walk toward him.

"I'm sorry I'm late," Rob said when he was close enough to be heard. The words were ordinary, and they sounded sincere. Surely it was only Anne's imagination that he seemed unwilling to meet her gaze. "I stopped at the post office," Rob continued. "It was my bad luck that Mr. Feltz was more garrulous than normal." The story was plausible. More than once Anne and Rob had joked about the postmaster's tendency to be as long-winded as the mayor. Perhaps there was nothing sinister in Rob's delay. "It wasn't a totally wasted time," he said, "because Mr. Feltz gave me a letter for you."

Though Rob smiled as he pronounced the words and handed the letter to Anne, the smile did not seem to reach his eyes. Once again, her heart plummeted with dismay. Something was bothering Rob, and Anne was afraid she knew what that something was.

She glanced at the postmark. New York! At least one thing had gone right today. She wouldn't have to write another letter to Dr. Muller, for this was his response. There was no question about it. Anne recognized the precise handwriting that she had seen so many times when the doctor had been treating her. Though she longed to rip open the envelope and read what he had written, Anne forced herself to slide it into her satchel as if it were of no more importance than an invitation to tea.

"Have you finished the design for the New York carousel?" she asked. When she had looked at the sketches, Rob had still been working on revisions to one horse, and he had told her he wasn't sure what type of rounding panels his patron wanted.

"Not quite," he said, "but Mark and Luke have started carving the chariots for your carousel." Ordinary words, an ordinary tone, and yet Rob's demeanor was anything but ordinary. Normally he and Anne walked side-by-side, not touching but close enough that their hands would occasionally brush. Whenever they would cross a street, Rob would place her hand on his arm. It was nothing more than a gentlemanly gesture. Anne certainly didn't need to be guided across the street, nor did she need physical support. But today Rob kept a marked distance between them, and when they crossed first Bridge and then River, his arm remained stiffly at his side rather than being bent as if inviting her hand to nestle in the crook of his elbow.

Actions speak louder than words. Anne couldn't count the number of times her mother had told her that, but never before had that homily seemed so appropriate. Though Rob said nothing, his actions made it clear how much had changed in less than a day. The easy camaraderie that they had enjoyed was gone, destroyed by a kiss that he obviously regretted. Rob was a gentleman, a kind and considerate person. No matter how awkward the situation, no matter how much he disliked it, he would not willingly hurt Anne. She knew that, just as she knew that he was struggling to hide his discomfort. She would have to be the one to release Rob from an unwanted obligation.

"I know you're anxious to get the small carousel finished," she said as they approached Fairlawn. It wasn't her imagination that Rob's pace was faster than normal. He wanted this walk to end. "I'll understand if you don't come to the nursery every day. I'm perfectly capable of walking home alone."

A moment of silence greeted her words. Rob turned to study her face, his own expression inscrutable. "That might be a good idea," he said at last.

Though his easy assent hurt more than she had dreamed possible, Anne nodded slowly. What else had she expected?

Pacing was foolish. Rob knew that. He had a carousel to build; he ought to be working on that. Pacing solved nothing. It merely wasted time that Rob could not afford to waste. And yet, here he was, striding from one end of the workshop to the other, making an abrupt turn and striding back. How foolish!

She regretted the kiss. The words echoed in Rob's mind with each step that he took. He clenched his fists, trying to bite back the bile that that realization brought. He had spent the day wondering what Anne would say when he joined her at the nursery. Would she speak of that magical moment when he'd held her in his arms and their lips had touched, or would she simply give him a special, knowing smile? Rob had imagined a dozen different things she might have said or done, but not once had he imagined what had actually happened.

Don't come to the nursery. The words reverberated louder than the gouge Luke had once dropped into a metal drum. Anne needed to say nothing more. It was clear that the kiss had been so distasteful to her that she didn't want to spend any time with Rob, lest he repeat his foolish action.

Rob turned and strode toward the door for what seemed like the millionth time. Didn't Anne know that walking home from the nursery with her was the highlight of his day? Didn't she know that he counted the hours until he would see her again? Didn't she know how much that kiss had meant to him? Of course she didn't! Anne had made her feelings obvious. Oh, she had done it in the nicest way possible, pretending that she was trying to help him. But only a total fool would misinterpret what she had said. *Stay away from me. I don't want to see you ever again.* That's what Anne had been saying, only she was too polite to phrase it that way.

Rob frowned. He had understood the message, and he would do what she had asked. He would finish the small carousel and the New York one as quickly as he could, and then he would move on. Somehow, somewhere he would build a life that didn't include Anne Moreland.

As he turned, Rob saw the envelope that he'd tossed on the table. At the time that he'd read it, he had dismissed its contents, knowing that working for a new carousel factory wasn't what he wanted. But now?

Now everything was different. Now the announcement that a fellow carver had sent him was the lifeline he needed. If the factory accepted him, he would be head carver. That was good. He would be able to design carousels without worrying about the business itself. That was even better. Best of all, the factory was on the other side of the state, hundreds of miles from Anne Moreland and dreams that would never come true.

Rob opened the envelope and reread the letter, then reached for a piece of paper. He would submit his application tonight. The sooner he left Hidden Falls, the better.

Though the path through the trees was still muddy, it would be faster than taking the road. Anne ran, heedless of the mud that covered her boots and was caking on her skirt. From the moment she had read Dr. Muller's response, she'd been filled with an overwhelming sense of urgency.

"What's wrong?" Susannah's eyes widened as she opened the door and saw Anne's bedraggled appearance.

"Nothing!" Anne forced the word out, then put a hand against her stomach, trying to slow her breathing. "It's good news, but I need your help." The words came out in bursts. "I think I've found Rob's sister."

Susannah raised one perfectly shaped eyebrow as she led Anne into the parlor. "Rob has a sister?"

As succinctly as she could, Anne explained how Rob and Edith had been separated and how important it was to him that he find Edith. "The name is different," Anne admitted as she concluded her story, "but there's a strong resemblance. That's why I think there's a good chance Delia is Edith. That's why I wrote to Dr. Muller." Anne pulled out the letter that Rob had given her that afternoon, never guessing that the contents concerned him. "The doctor says Delia married one of their patients, and they're living in Saratoga."

"Which is less than a day's journey from here." Susannah finished the sentence. As the two dogs scampered into the room, obviously curious to see who was visiting, she scooped Pepper into her arms. Salt sniffed at Anne's boots. "That's good news for Rob," Susannah said. "What I don't understand is why you need my help."

Giving in to the inevitable, Anne lifted the white dog into her lap and scratched between its ears. "Even though they have the same shape eyes, Delia may not be Rob's sister. I think she is, but I don't want to raise his hopes and then have him disappointed." Anne looked at her sister-in-law. "Oh, Susannah, if you could have seen Rob's expression when he told me about Edith and how much he wanted to see her again, you'd know how important this is."

Susannah nodded. "I understand." Something in her expression told Anne that she wasn't referring only to Rob's desire to be reunited with his sister. Surely Susannah didn't know how Anne felt about Rob. "What do you want to do?"

"I thought you and I could go to Saratoga." Anne had two reasons for inviting Susannah. In addition to the fact that propriety kept her from traveling alone, she needed Susannah's talent. "Of course, we wouldn't tell anyone why we're going," she continued. "We can claim that I want to experience one of those healing springs or that you need to paint something there." Anne didn't care what pretense they used. "I want to ask Delia what she remembers of her childhood, and — if it seems likely that she's Rob's sister — I thought you could make a sketch of her for Rob."

Susannah's eyes narrowed for an instant. "Wouldn't it be easier to simply send this woman a letter, asking about her childhood?"

"It might be easier," and Anne had considered that approach, "but letters get lost, and it takes time to get a response." Anne didn't want to go through the same delays she'd experienced waiting for Dr. Muller's reply. "Besides," she added, "Delia might not feel comfortable writing to me. I might never get an answer." As Salt squirmed, Anne set him on the floor. "The truth is, Susannah, Charles has always accused me of being impatient, and this time he's right. I don't want to wait."

With a sigh that might have been resignation, Susannah asked when Anne wanted to leave.

"Tomorrow."

"I can't be ready that soon. Not unless you want me to tell Charles the real reason we're going to Saratoga."

Anne shook her head, finally agreeing with Susannah that they would leave in three days. "That will give me time to talk to Ralph," she said, trying to find something positive about the delay.

Once again Susannah's eyes widened. "Now you've confused me. Why do you need a lawyer's advice about talking to Rob's sister?"

"It's not that. I think Rob needs to incorporate his business. That would give him more protection and people might take him more seriously. Ralph can help me with that."

"I see." Susannah's smile made Anne wonder just what it was that her sister-in-law saw.

It was a day of changes. That morning for the first time, Anne left Bertha in charge of the children while she consulted Ralph Chambers. "You'll be here alone when I go to Saratoga," she told her assistant, claiming that Susannah wanted to see the city and had asked Anne to accompany her. As Bertha began to protest, Anne held up a hand. "Nonsense. Of course you're capable. You're so good with the children, they won't even know that I'm gone." Though it was nothing less than the truth, Bertha's face had shone with pleasure, and that made Anne smile. Though she might not see her own dreams come true, she would do her best to help others achieve theirs.

Bertha's grin was so infectious that not even the gray day seemed to affect the children. But at the end of the day, Bertha's smile faded. "Where's Rob?" she asked as Anne closed the door behind them and there was no sight of the carousel carver. "I'm surprised he's late again."

He wasn't late; he simply wasn't coming. "He's trying to finish a new merry-go-round." Anne tried to bite back her disappointment. Despite everything she had said, she had hoped that Rob would ignore her suggestion and would come to the nursery to walk home with her. The fact that he didn't was added proof of how much he regretted his impulsive kiss. She shouldn't have been surprised; she shouldn't have been disappointed; she shouldn't allow her heart to ache. But hearts, Anne knew, didn't always behave the way they should. And that would make her next conversation with him all the more difficult.

Anne took a deep breath as she approached the workshop. *This was business, strictly business,* she told herself. There was no reason to feel nervous about discussing business with Rob. As Anne entered the converted stable, she saw that Mark and Luke were there, working on the small chariots. *Excellent!* Their presence reduced the awkwardness of talking to Rob.

"I spoke with Ralph Chambers," she told Rob after she had admired the progress Mark and Luke had made. She would not — she absolutely would not — tell Rob how much she had missed his company on the walk home. "Ralph agrees that it would be wise for you to incorporate." Without waiting for Rob's response, Anne explained the reasons, ending with, "Ralph will be happy to file the applications for you."

On the opposite side of the workshop Mark and Luke kept up a steady banter as they sharpened their gouges. Rob seemed oblivious to his assistants' joking and the occasional screech of a gouge on the stone. "It's very kind of you to consult an attorney," he said when Anne had finished her explanations, his voice as dispassionate as if he were addressing a total stranger.

A lump formed in Anne's throat. This wasn't the response she had expected. In the past, though he'd freely admitted that the details of running the business did not excite him, Rob had always been enthusiastic about Anne's plans. What had changed?

Before Anne could ask the question, Rob spoke. "I appreciate all that you've done, but there will not be a Ludlow Carousel Company."

The lump in Anne's throat expanded, and though she swallowed, trying desperately to dislodge it, it would not move. *No carousel company! What had happened to change Rob's mind, and why, oh why, did he sound so dispassionate?* Rob might as well have been reciting multiplication tables for all the emotion she heard in his voice. Where was the Rob she knew, the one who wanted to be independent, the one who wanted to create his own company?

"Why not?" she asked, forcing the words past the lump that seemed to have reached boulder size.

Rob shrugged, his face betraying no more expression than a piece of wood. "That was a dream, nothing else. The reality is, I'm not cut out to run my own business. I should have realized that months ago."

His tone left no doubt of the futility of arguing. Rob had made his decision, and nothing would sway him. Why? Why had he changed so drastically? This was a side of Rob Anne had never seen. The Rob she had known had been enthusiastic, he'd been sad, he'd been angry, but he had never been apathetic. Anne's mind whirled, trying to find a cause.

"This is because of Edith, isn't it?" That was the only reason she could imagine for his change of heart. It couldn't have anything to do with the night he had kissed her. Rob might regret that, and his actions seemed to indicate that he did, but he would never change his life plans because of Anne. She wasn't that important to him. It had to be Edith. Rob's worries about her were clouding his judgment. "What if you found your sister?"

Rob shrugged again. "That doesn't appear very likely, but it wouldn't make any difference even if I did find Edith. I know who I am and what I can do."

This was the problem. Something had made Rob doubt his own abilities. Anne couldn't imagine what it was, but at this point, that didn't matter. What did was restoring Rob's confidence. "You can do anything you want."

He scuffed the floor with his shoe, then raised his eyes to meet Anne's. What she saw chilled her more than anything he had said. His eyes were devoid of expression, dull and lifeless. "Maybe I don't want my own company. Maybe that was your dream, not mine."

Anne had never believed that hearts could break. Now she knew how wrong she had been.

CHAPTER TEN

Anne broke the chocolate into the pan, then measured the sugar and milk. Though she shuddered when she lit the stove and the ring of flames appeared, she placed the saucepan on the burner and began to stir the mixture. Perhaps it was silly to think that cocoa would comfort her, but today that was all she had.

As a child when she had skinned her knee, once the scrape was cleaned and bandaged, Mama would draw her into her arms and rock her, whispering words of comfort. When her stomach ached, Mrs. Enke would make peppermint tea, serving it in the special oversized cup that she called the "healing mug." And the time Anne had broken her arm, her father had left the mill to hold her other hand while Dr. Kellogg set the fracture. Today was different. Today there was no one to comfort her. Mama and Papa were gone, and Mrs. Enke was visiting a friend. Though Anne knew Charles and Susannah would listen to her and provide sympathy, she didn't want to intrude on their privacy. It would be unfair to disturb their last evening together, since it was because of Anne that they would be parted for the first time in their marriage.

The person Anne longed for most was Jane. In the past, she and Jane had shared each other's joys and sorrows. With the intuition that twins often shared, there had been times when they had had an almost uncanny knowledge of what had befallen the other. Jane would have understood that even though Anne's pain had no physical cause, it was nonetheless real. But since they had returned from Europe, the closeness they had once shared had disappeared. However Jane was spending her days — and Anne suspected that whatever she was doing involved Matt Wagner — she chose not to confide her thoughts, her dreams, even her disappointments in her sister. And so Anne stood in the kitchen, stirring a pan of cocoa, hoping that the delicious smelling beverage would help calm her turbulent thoughts.

When the chocolate had melted, Anne pulled the pan from the burner, carefully extinguishing the fire, then poured the liquid into Mrs. Enke's special mug. Tonight she needed all the help she could get. When she had fled the workshop, Anne had tried not to think, but the memory of Rob's words would not be extinguished as easily as the stove's flame. No matter what she did, she saw his face, heard his voice, and shuddered at the realization that she had failed again.

Anne wrapped her hands around the mug, seeking comfort from the inanimate object, then took a sip. By the time she had drained the cup, the cocoa had warmed her, dispelling the chill that had settled deep inside her when Rob had fixed that steady, emotionless gaze on her. But, though Anne was no longer shivering, nothing could heal the ache in her heart.

She was alone tonight. She would always be alone. She climbed the stairs to her room, blinking back the tears. Ever since the fire, she had known that was her destiny, and she thought she had accepted it. But when she had returned to Hidden Falls, Anne had started to dream again. That was a mistake. She had been a fool to dream that she could make a difference in other people's lives. She had been a fool to dream that she could have a "happily ever after." She had been a fool to dream of anything at all. But Anne had dreamed, and now she had to face the reality that those dreams would never come true. It would have been better — far better — if she had not let herself dream.

The nightmare came again that night. At first it was like every other time. Anne smelled the smoke, felt the flames, faced the bone-chilling realization that no matter what she did, no matter how hard she tried, she would not reach them in time. But then the horror changed, and she knew that this time was different. This time there were three people behind the wall of flames, three people she needed to save. Her despair grew. She must succeed. She must.

Though it felt as if she ran for hours and made no progress, at last Anne reached her parents' room. She crawled along the floor, trying to find the bed. Mama and Papa were there. She knew that. As tears coursed down her cheeks, she dragged first one, then the other onto the balcony. But there was someone else in the room. There was a third person she needed to save. Where was he? The smoke burned her throat; sparks landed on her arms; her face felt as if it were on fire. Where was he? Where was the third person? It was desperately important that she find him. She couldn't leave him with the smoke and the flames. She had to get him to safety. As the ceiling began to cave in, Anne screamed. *Rob! Where was Rob?* She screamed again.

"It's all right, Anne." She felt the warm arms encircle her, heard the soothing words, and slowly she returned to the present. "It was only a nightmare."

Anne opened her eyes. Jane was kneeling beside her bed, trying to calm her as she had done so many times in the past year. "It was only a dream," her sister said.

But Jane didn't know how real the dreams seemed and how the terror they brought was worse than that horrible night. Jane didn't know that this dream differed from the others, that it was more than reliving the past. Jane didn't know that this dream threatened the man Anne loved.

"When will they end?" Anne asked.

Her sister shook her head slowly. "I wish I knew."

It was the throbbing of her head that awakened her. Anne grimaced with pain as she swung her legs off the bed. It was always the same. Though the terror that accompanied the nightmare would fade, the aching of her head served as a reminder that her sleep had been disturbed. Fortunately, the pain would dissipate after two cups of strong coffee.

An hour later when the pounding in her head had been reduced to no more than a light tapping, Anne stood in front of her wardrobe, trying to decide which clothing to pack. She and Susannah were leaving on the afternoon train, and though they would be gone only a few days, they needed to be prepared for autumn's changeable weather. She would take . . . Mrs. Enke's knocking interrupted Anne's planning. "He's here again." Anne had no need to ask her guest's identity. There was only one person who made Mrs. Enke's lips purse with such disapproval.

Anne sighed. Though she had no time to visit with Philip, a lifetime of training in the importance of good manners told her she could not refuse. That would be rude, and rudeness was a cardinal sin in the Moreland household. Still, her feet moved reluctantly as they propelled her toward the parlor. Seeing Philip would be awkward. No matter what he said or did, Anne couldn't forget that Jane believed he was courting her.

Today for the first time since the Harrods' party, both of Philip's hands rested at his sides. Anne managed a small smile. At least he had not brought a gift. She would consider that a good omen. Perhaps he had learned that she was going to Saratoga and had come to bid her a safe journey.

Refusing her offer of refreshments, Philip settled on the chair opposite Anne and cleared his throat. "My dear, I hope my words will not come as a surprise to you." His voice was as calm and almost as emotionless as Rob's had been. There was no need for Anne to dread what Philip might say next. He reached for her hands and clasped them in his. "I believe you are aware of the high regard in which I hold you. I believe you know that if your parents were still alive, their deepest desire would be for you to be happy. I share that desire." Philip cleared his throat again. "My dear, will you do me the honor of becoming my wife?"

Anne should have been prepared for Philip's question, and yet she wasn't. She had known Philip was courting her and that he might some day ask her to marry him. She had even debated what her answer would be. But she had never thought that her first proposal would be like this. This wasn't the way Anne had envisioned a man asking for her hand. Where was the moonlight? Where were the flowers? Most of all, where was the declaration of love? A sense of outrage that was quickly superseded by disappointment

219

swept through her. The only man who wanted to marry her didn't even pretend to love her.

Philip squeezed her hands, reminding her that he was waiting for an answer. Anne knew what he expected, and perhaps he was right. Perhaps she should marry him. Though there was no love between them, she could assuage Philip's loneliness, and she would no longer be alone. It would be a sensible move. Anne took a deep breath, trying to chase away the image of a small house, a picket fence, and a little boy who looked like Rob. Though it meant that she would spend the rest of her life alone, being a maiden aunt to Charles's and Jane's children, Anne could not be sensible.

"I'm sorry, Philip." Where were the pretty speeches she and Jane had rehearsed, the gentle methods they had devised for politely refusing unwanted suitors? Now, when she needed them, Anne could not recall a single word. "I'm sorry," she repeated, "but I cannot marry you."

Releasing her hands, Philip rose to his feet. His fists were clenched, and lines of anger bracketed his mouth as he glared down at her. "Why not?" he demanded. "I can give you everything you need. You'll have a house as fine as Fairlawn and servants to care for it. You'll have beautiful clothes and jewelry. We can travel anywhere you wish." Philip took a deep breath, exhaling slowly as if he were trying to control his fury. "And then there are children," he said in a softer voice. "Don't you want children of your own?"

She did. Oh! how she did. But children were only part of what she wanted. Philip had provided a list of everything he thought she needed. Anne knew they were things most women dreamed of having, and they would, she admitted, make life pleasant. Though Philip's list might have enticed another woman, it left Anne with a deep sense of emptiness, for he had never mentioned the one thing she truly needed: love. Without love she could not marry him.

Anne rose to her feet. "Please do not think me ungrateful," she said, finally remembering some of the speeches she and Jane had rehearsed. "Though I wish I could give you a different answer, I cannot marry you, Philip. You're a dear friend, but I don't love you."

His lips thinned again. "I have enough love for both of us, Mary."

A shiver raced down Anne's spine. This was the second time Philip had called her by her mother's name. "I'm not Mary."

He blinked, and as he did, Anne saw the confusion in his eyes. "Of course you're not Mary. She died." He was silent for a moment. "Perhaps my proposal came as a surprise to you," he said at last. "I understand that you may need time to consider all that I have offered. Take some time. A day or two, a week, even a month. I'm certain you will change your mind."

"I won't change my mind," Anne said as gently as she could.

Muttering an oath, Philip stalked out of the house.

Anne sank onto the chair, feeling as if her legs would no longer support her. What a dreadful morning! Though anger had colored Philip's words, Anne knew that he was hurt as well as angry. It was the hurt that made her heart ache. Oh, how she hated to hurt anyone! Both of her parents had stressed the need to make people happy. "Always consider the other person's feelings," her mother had admonished. "Try not to bruise those feelings, for they are more tender than a newly sprouted blade of grass. If you trample them, they will be destroyed."

Anne had failed to save Philip's feelings, just as she had failed so many times before. She had failed to save her parents. Somehow she had failed Jane, for the closeness they had shared was gone. She had failed to help Rob create his own company. No matter what she did, she failed everyone she loved. The only thing that was left was to find Rob's sister. She would not fail at that. Resolutely, Anne climbed the stairs to her room.

But, five minutes later as she stood staring at the open wardrobe, she realized that she wasn't thinking clearly. She couldn't make a simple decision about which clothing to pack. Instead, she vacillated, touching one skirt, then moving to the next, while images of Philip's angry face paraded through her mind. Susannah had once confided that when she was haunted by memories, she would paint. Anne wasn't a painter. The only thing she knew that brought the kind of calm Susannah had described was being with Rob's painted ponies.

Anne pulled out her watch. It was the time of the morning when Rob and his assistants took a break, leaving the workshop empty for a few minutes. No one would bother her if she slipped in for a few minutes. She hurried down the back stairway and across the lawn. Once inside the workshop, she moved instinctively to Lillian, the lead horse for the new carousel. Though still unpainted, the mare's flowing mane and the proud tilt of her head had drawn Anne from the first time she had seen them. This was a horse that would never admit defeat. Unlike Anne, Lillian radiated strength.

She wrapped her arms around the horse's neck and laid her head against it. And as she did, Anne began to sob. She cried for the loss of her parents. She cried for the barriers that had grown between her and Jane. Most of all, she cried for dreams that would never come true, dreams that had once included Rob.

"Anne!" In her torrent of tears and sobs she had not heard him enter the workshop. "What's wrong?"

Anne took a deep breath before she faced Rob. "Nothing."

He shook his head and, wrapping his arm around her shoulders, gently drew her toward the one comfortable chair in the workshop. "You can't expect me to believe that nothing's wrong," he said as he settled her into the chair. "Your wet cheeks tell a different story." His voice was warm and comforting, far different from the steely coldness of last night. This was the old Rob, the Rob who had been her friend.

He pulled up a stool and sat next to her. "What's wrong?" he repeated. When Anne said nothing, Rob laid his hand on hers. It wasn't only his words that were warm and comforting. The warmth of his hand began to seep into her, melting the ice that had clogged her veins, chasing some of her despair. "You'll feel better if you talk," Rob said.

She couldn't talk. She couldn't tell Rob how many times she had failed.

"Trust me," Rob said. "Remember that volcanoes need to vent."

Anne took another deep breath, remembering the time she had had a boil on her arm. It had hurt so much that wearing even a light sleeve was agony. Mama had insisted that the boil had to be lanced. "Yes, that will hurt," she had told Anne, "but it's the only way. You have to let the poison out so that the healing will begin." Perhaps this was like that. Perhaps talking was like lancing the boil.

Anne closed her eyes for a moment, trying to muster the courage to put her pain into words. "I feel like such a failure."

Though she spoke so softly that she wasn't certain he heard her, Rob's response was instantaneous. "You are not a failure!" He enunciated each word slowly and carefully. As he paused, Anne watched anger flit across his face. It was gone a second later, but the fervor in his voice told her it still seethed. "Who made you think you were a failure?" he demanded.

"It's not who, it's what." Anne held out her hand and began to count, turning down one finger. "The nursery children would rather be with Bertha than me." A second finger. "I couldn't help you set up your company." A third.

But before she could list the third reason, Rob interrupted. He took her hand in his and straightened out the fingers. "Let's talk about this." Though his expression was solemn, warmth radiated from his eyes. "We'll start with the children. I've seen the way they respond to you. They're happy to be with you, Anne."

"But they're different with Bertha." Anne brushed an errant tear from her cheek.

Rob nodded. "That's probably true, but I doubt it's for the reason you think. Have you ever considered that the children might be in awe of you? After all, you're a Moreland. Their parents work for your brother. Don't you think they know that? Even though you would never ask Charles to fire one of their parents if a child misbehaved, they may not realize that."

Rob entwined his fingers with hers. In all likelihood, he did it unconsciously, not knowing that the simple gesture warmed Anne more than his words. While their fingers were laced, Anne was not alone.

"Bertha's different," Rob continued. "She's like one of them, so the children can relax a bit more with her."

"It was kind of you to say that." Though Rob's theory was plausible, Anne wasn't convinced that it was the reason for the children's preference. Rob had seen how distraught Anne was; this was his attempt to calm her.

"That wasn't kindness. It was the truth." Rob tightened his grip on her hand. "As for the Ludlow Carousel Company, I told you that the problem isn't you. It's me. I'm a carver, not an entrepreneur." He gestured toward the small table where a pile of papers appeared on the verge of toppling over. Surely he hadn't been rummaging through the files Anne had so carefully arranged.

"I could help you." That was what Anne wanted to do. It was where her talents lay. She was good at organization and planning. Though she couldn't carve an animal anyone would recognize, she could help Rob turn his talent into a commercial success.

"That would be possible only if I stayed here." Rob's eyes darkened with something that looked like pain. His expression reminded Anne of the times he'd spoken of Edith, and for a second she was tempted to tell him that his sister might be only a few hours away. Anne kept her lips firmly pressed together, refusing to expose Rob to yet another disappointment.

Gently he untwined their fingers and placed Anne's hand on the chair arm. "Anne, I can't remain in Hidden Falls." There was no doubt about it. Rob's voice betrayed the anguish he was feeling. Anne was certain that pain was related to his sister. Searching for Edith was the reason he had to leave Hidden Falls. But the answer was so close. Delia had to be Edith. She simply had to! Once Rob was reunited with his sister, he could stay here.

As if he heard her thoughts, Rob shook his head. "It wouldn't work out. Besides, you'll be married soon, and once that happens, you won't have time to worry about an itinerant carousel carver."

Anne felt the blood drain from her face. Why was Rob speaking of marriage? "I'm not going to marry. I refused Philip." The instant the words were out of her mouth, Anne regretted them. Rob didn't need to know about Philip's proposal. No one did. She wasn't proud of the fact that she had hurt another person's feelings. That was yet another failure.

"You're wrong." Once again Rob's expression was inscrutable. "You'll marry, Anne. I know you will. If ever there was a woman who was meant to marry, it's you."

Anne stared at Rob, trying to make sense of his words. They had been talking about his carousel company, and suddenly the conversation had veered to marriage. She didn't understand why that had happened unless Rob somehow knew the reason for Philip's visit. "Are you saying I should have accepted Philip's proposal?" Anne asked at last. Rob might not love her, but she knew that he regarded her as a friend. Was this a friend's advice?

For a long moment Rob said nothing. Instead, he stared at the floor as if the wood shavings and paint chips held the answer to Anne's question. When he raised his eyes to hers, the pain she had seen before appeared to have intensified. "I didn't say that. I simply said that you were meant to marry." Though his eyes radiated pain, Rob's voice was neutral, once again devoid of any emotion.

Anne swallowed deeply as the import of his words registered. Rob hadn't told her to marry Philip, but he also hadn't advised her to refuse him. The reason was obvious. If he harbored any tender sentiments — oh, why mince words? — if Rob loved her, he would have insisted that she not marry Philip.

Fighting back her tears, Anne rose and returned to the house. If she had had any doubts about Rob's feelings for her, his words dissolved them. Rob saw her as a friend, nothing more.

She was gone. Rob dipped a brush into the paint, taking care to put exactly the right amount of paint on the tip. Though his life might be in shambles, this horse would turn out perfectly, or as close to perfect as he could make it. The small carousel was the last thing he would give Anne, and Rob was determined that it would have no imperfections.

He looked across the room at Mark and Luke. They were putting the finishing touches on the chariots, joking as if this were an ordinary day, not one where there was no possibility of a visit from Anne. Rob outlined the saddle. It was strange how empty the days seemed, knowing that he would not see Anne. No one seemed certain how long she would be gone, though the fact that she and Susannah had boarded the afternoon train had fueled the rumor mill's speculations.

Rob squinted slightly, looking at the horse. The saddle needed a little more ocher. Why hadn't Anne told him she was leaving? She had been right here in the workshop only an hour before she'd gone to the depot. It might have been because she was so upset. That was the most palatable possibility. Rob wished he could believe that was the cause, but he suspected the real reason she hadn't confided in him was that Anne hadn't thought it important for him to know that she was going away.

As distasteful as that possibility was, there was one that was much worse. Rob was afraid that Anne had not made the decision to leave Hidden Falls until after her visit to the workshop. Charles claimed that Susannah wanted to sketch the baths at Saratoga and that she had asked Anne to accompany her. It was a plausible story and Rob might have believed it if Philip Biddle had not left Hidden Falls this morning. That might be coincidence. Philip's destination might not be Saratoga.

Rob mixed ocher into the paint, nodding slightly when the saddle's hue was the one he had sought. He wanted to believe that Philip's departure was not connected to Anne's, but he couldn't. Not when he knew that Philip had asked Anne to marry him. Not when he knew how determined Philip Biddle could be. Especially not when Rob had been fool enough to tell Anne she ought to marry.

Though Rob's thoughts were whirling faster than an out of control merry-go-round, his hand remained steady. No matter what he wanted to believe, what his heart told him was that Anne had listened to him and that she had reconsidered Philip's proposal of marriage. He believed that Philip was going to Saratoga to marry Anne.

Rob finished painting the saddle. It was beautiful. The thought of Anne and Philip together was not. Try though he might to block the images, Rob could not dismiss the picture of Anne and Philip walking into that ugly pile of stone that Philip called a house, Philip's arms around Anne's slender waist, his head bending to press a kiss on . . . *Stop it!* Rob told himself. *You have no right to be jealous.* He nodded slowly. His conscience was right. If Anne married Philip, it was partially his fault. After all, Rob had been the one who had encouraged her to marry.

A burst of laughter on the other side of the room told Rob his assistants were enjoying their work. They weren't haunted by visions of Anne and Philip together the way he was. Rob reached for the black paint. He needed to focus on the horse, not Anne. So what if she married? It wasn't as if he had any intention of marrying her himself. No matter what Rob felt for her, that wouldn't be fair to Anne.

He outlined the first hoof, his hand steadier than his heart. It was pounding erratically, distressed by the thought of Anne's marriage. He shouldn't let himself care. Even if by some miracle he found Edith, Rob couldn't marry Anne. How could he ask her to take a chance on a man with an uncertain future? Rob's mood was as black as the paint he was applying. The answer was simple: Anne deserved more than he could offer. Rob couldn't and wouldn't ask her to settle for less. And because he wouldn't do that, he also shouldn't be one of those proverbial dogs in the manger, preventing others from having something he didn't want.

Anne deserved happiness. She would make some man a wonderful wife. But Philip? Rob gritted his teeth.

CHAPTER ELEVEN

"Hey, boss man."

Rob frowned at Mark. "You know I don't like that title." While it was true that Mark and Luke worked for him, he preferred to think of them as partners, not employees. After all, they all had roles to play in creating a carousel, and none was more important that the other.

Normally he wouldn't have said anything to Mark about the hated title, but nothing had been normal since Anne had left. Was she even now honeymooning with Philip? Rob gripped his paintbrush tightly enough to emboss his fingerprints on it.

"Okay, head man." Rob's lips quirked in a wry smile. That was one title he couldn't deny, for he was the man who carved the horses' heads. He raised an eyebrow, encouraging Mark to continue. "What are we gonna do next?" Mark asked.

"Good question." Luke paused in his

painting and turned toward Rob. "We gonna stay here?"

It was early morning, the time when Mark and Luke frequently rode Susannah's horses. Today, however, the three men were in the workshop, trying to finish another coat of paint before breakfast. The engine and cranks for the small merry-go-round were scheduled to arrive within a week, and they wanted to have all the animals completed before then. They had already moved some of the finished horses outside to the platform where they would assemble and test the carousel, freeing more space in the workshop for the meticulous job of painting.

"Do you want to stay?" Rob had learned that when you didn't have any answers, it was wise to counter one question with another. Although in this case, he wasn't certain he would like the reply. In the past, both Mark and Luke had told him that they enjoyed the itinerant life, but the tenor of their questions made Rob suspect that they'd changed their minds.

Mark dipped his brush into green paint and began to outline the seahorse. "There's this right pretty girl at the mill," he said. "Jeannie's her name. And . . ." He ducked his head, as if the side of the chariot was the most fascinating object on earth.

"Mark here's got it bad," Luke explained. "We figured, seeing as how you're sparking Miss Anne . . ."

Rob didn't let him finish his thought. "I'm not sparking Anne." Though he had encouraged a camaraderie with the men, there were certain topics that were off limits. Anne Moreland was one of them.

Mark raised his head and gave Rob a long appraising look. "If you say so."

"I do." Rob flinched. His choice of words couldn't have been worse, for those two short syllables conjured images he had been trying to ignore, images of Anne and Philip saying those words to each other.

Rob clenched his fists as he walked into town. The excuse he used was that the morning mail should have arrived, but mostly he needed to escape the workshop. The situation was worse than he'd thought if Mark and Luke — not the most observant of men — recognized that he harbored more than friendly feelings for Anne.

Rob increased his pace, as if physical exertion could solve his problems. He had been so certain that he'd hidden his emotions. There was, he had told himself, no way that anyone would guess that he dreamed of Anne every night and that thoughts of her filled much of his days. It appeared that he was wrong, and that was a problem. A big problem. The last thing Rob wanted was to have anyone in Hidden Falls gossiping about Anne. It would be even worse if she married Philip. The rumor mill would feed on a story of unrequited love. Anne didn't deserve that. Indeed, she didn't. Rob turned onto Main Street and approached the post office. The best thing he could do, perhaps the only thing he could do, was to leave Hidden Falls. Soon. And if that didn't please Mark and Luke, well . . . Anne was more important than his assistants.

Rob's mood did not improve when he entered the small red brick building that housed Hidden Falls' post office. Although all he wanted was to escape, Mr. Feltz was more garrulous than normal, holding Rob's three letters in his hand as he speculated about the reason Miss Anne and Miss Susannah had gone to Saratoga and why Philip Biddle had driven out of town the next morning. It was only after repeated assurances that Rob had no information about the travelers that the postmaster handed him his mail. If he had needed additional proof that he could not subject Anne to further gossip, the time with Mr. Feltz had provided it.

Rob glanced at the envelopes as he left the store but waited until he was in the park before he opened them. There was no need to fuel the postmaster's rumors by admitting how anxious he was for mail. By now he suspected everyone in town knew about the number of letters he wrote and received, but despite repeated questions, Rob had not satisfied Mr. Feltz's curiosity about the content of those letters. He wouldn't start today.

Though there were benches in the park, Rob had no desire to sit. Some news was easier to take standing. The first two letters had come from the small town in Ohio that had been his last lead. Striding toward the carousel, Rob tore them open. As always, hope and fear mingled as he withdrew the sheets of paper. Though he was anxious to read the contents, he was also fearful that these, like all the previous inquiries he had made, had been for naught. Rob's fears were well-founded. Both the mayor and the minister reported that there were no records of a Barton family in their town.

Stuffing the envelopes into his pocket, Rob walked around the carousel. Soon the workers would enclose the pavilion, protecting the horses from the winter weather. Rob wouldn't be here to see that. He'd be somewhere else, carving another horse, sending out dozens more letters about Edith and waiting for the inevitable responses. Inevitable. Rob stopped in mid stride and stared at the lead horse. When had he started believing that the quest was hopeless? Though he'd frequently been discouraged, never before had he let himself think that he might not succeed.

Rob touched the Cherni figure of Anne's doll, remembering the pleasure in her eyes when she had seen it. While the doll represented part of her past, not long after that day Anne had told him that she had finally accepted her inability to change the past and her need to focus on the future. Though Anne hadn't been advising him, perhaps he should adopt her philosophy. Perhaps it was time for Rob to face the fact that he would never find Edith. Perhaps he should admit that being reunited with his sister was one more dream that would never come true.

Rob sighed. He wasn't ready. Not yet. He would send out one more set of letters, and then, if they, too, produced only dead ends, he would accept the loss of his sister.

He sat on the platform next to the lead horse and pulled the third letter from his pocket. He'd been surprised when he recognized the postmark and realized that the answer had come by return mail. In Rob's experience, rapid replies brought only bad news. That was why, even though he had been almost as anxious for this letter as for the ones about Edith, he hesitated to open the envelope. A man could take only so much bad news in any one day.

A squirrel scampered by, its cheeks bulging with acorns. The furry animal was prepared for the future; Rob should be, too. He slid his finger under the flap, then slowly withdrew the sheet of paper. As his eyes scanned the words, they widened. He read the few lines once, then again, not quite believing what he saw. The owners of the new carousel factory, far from rejecting his application as he had feared, had offered him the position of head carver. The wages they'd proposed were more generous than Rob had expected, and they had even agreed that he could bring his assistants with him.

This was the answer to his problems: a new and exciting job in a city far away from Anne Moreland. Why then, did he feel as if the sun had just disappeared, never to return?

The house was tiny, probably no more than three rooms, but the freshly painted shut-

ters and picket fence, as well as the im-
maculately groomed flower beds, told Anne
that the owners cherished it and saw it as a
home rather than simply a house. To her
surprise, Anne experienced a jolt of envy.
Though she lived in a building many times
the size of this, since her parents' death, it
had been nothing more than a place to sleep
and eat. How wonderful it would be to have
a real home . . . and a man to share it. A
man like Rob.

Pushing those thoughts firmly aside, Anne
reached for Susannah's hand, then took a
deep breath and knocked on the door. Her
own dreams didn't matter today; what was
important was helping Rob's come true.
Please, please, she prayed silently. *Please
let Delia be Edith. Please don't let this be
another dead end.* Anne tightened her grip
on Susannah's hand, trying to keep hers
from trembling as she waited for someone
to answer the knock. Though it seemed like
an eternity, it was only a few moments
before the door opened and the blond
woman Anne remembered from Dr.
Muller's office stood before them.

"Can I help you?" she asked, obviously
perplexed by the unexpected arrival of two
women. It was clear that she did not recognize Anne.

Anne nodded slightly. Delia looked the way she remembered her, and yet there were differences. It wasn't simply that her clothing and hairstyle were less formal. Though her features were the same, Delia's face bore a glow of happiness that had not been there in New York. And then there was the most dramatic change. The woman who stood before her was with child. Anne did not claim to be an expert on pregnancy, but she guessed that the baby was due in less than a month.

"I'm not sure you remember me, Mrs. Webster," Anne said, trying not to stare at the face that looked so much like Rob's. The resemblance was even stronger than Anne had remembered. "I'm Anne Moreland. I was one of Dr. Muller's patients."

The woman nodded slowly as she took a step closer, those familiar blue eyes searching Anne's face for clues to her identity. "I recognize your voice, but . . ."

"My face is different." Anne completed the sentence. "Sometimes I'm still startled when I glance in the mirror."

The woman gave Anne another long look. "Won't you come in?" she said at last. "I'm afraid I cannot stand too long." Delia Webster, the woman who might be Rob's sister, laid a protective hand on her stomach. "The doctor says I'm having twins."

Anne introduced Susannah as the two women followed Delia into the house. As Anne had surmised, there was one large room that served as kitchen, parlor, and dining room, while two closed doors led to what she guessed were bedrooms. Though the furnishings were simple, the central room radiated comfort. Anne and Susannah took seats on the sofa while Delia chose a straight-backed chair.

"I imagine that you're wondering why I'm here," Anne said when their hostess was settled.

Delia brushed back her hair in a gesture that Anne remembered. "I worked with many patients, but no one has sought me out once they left the clinic. That's why I don't imagine this is a social call."

Are you Rob Ludlow's sister? Though that was the question Anne wanted to ask, if she blurted it out, Delia would think she had lost her mind as well as her beauty.

"You have lovely eyes," she said. "The shape is very unusual."

Although those eyes now reflected confusion, as if she wondered why two women would travel to Saratoga to discuss the shape of her features, Delia nodded. "I inherited them from my mother. But," Delia continued, "I still don't understand why you're here. It's not that you're unwelcome, but . . ."

Anne seized the opening. "A friend of mine was separated from his sister when they were both young children. He's spent years trying to find her. The reason we're here is that his eyes are the same shape and color as yours."

"So you think I might be that sister." Once more Delia laid her hand on her stomach in a protective gesture.

"I do." Though her name wasn't Edith, there was such a strong resemblance to Rob that Anne could not believe this wasn't his sister. She even had the same cleft in her chin.

"I truly hate to disappoint you and your friend," Delia said, "but I was an only child."

Anne wouldn't believe it. She couldn't. Surely Delia was mistaken. Though she had been raised apart from Rob, wouldn't her foster parents have told her of his existence? For a moment the only sounds in the room were the ticking of the clock and the three women's breathing. "Were you born in Philadelphia?" Anne asked, trying desperately to find a hole in Delia's story.

Anne's former nurse frowned. "I don't

know. My birth certificate was destroyed in a fire, and we moved so often when I was a child that I don't have any distinct memories of the first few years. The towns all blurred."

Anne tried not to sigh. No wonder Rob had had difficulty tracing his sister if her new family led such a peripatetic life. She couldn't give up. "Rob's sister was named Edith. Edith Ludlow. She was born in Philadelphia but was only a small child when their parents died." Though Delia listened politely, it was obvious that she did not believe Edith Ludlow's story was hers. "Rob was sent to live with his father's brother, and Edith was taken in by their mother's sister." Anne frowned, wondering why she hadn't asked Rob what the aunt's last name was. Delia's name before she married had been Barclay. Though Susannah said nothing, she laid a comforting hand on Anne's arm.

"I wish I could help you." Delia's regret sounded sincere. "I know I would hate it if my children were ever separated, and I'd want to think that anyone who could would help them be reunited." Delia touched her stomach again. "One of the reasons I'm so happy that I'm having twins is that I've always longed for a sister or brother. No matter how much I hoped for a baby sister or brother, there were none." Her lips curved in a self-deprecating smile, the same smile Anne had often seen on Rob's face. "My mother said I was her miracle child. They'd given up hope of having children, and then I came."

It was an unusual choice of words, but Anne said nothing until she and Susannah were back in their hotel room. "I believe she's Rob's sister," she told Susannah. "She simply doesn't know it." And that was so very frustrating. Anne had hoped to find Rob's sister. Instead, she had reached what appeared to be another dead end.

Susannah looked up from her sketching and nodded. "I agree. I suppose they could be cousins, but the resemblance is almost too strong for that."

Unable to sit still, Anne rose and parted the drapes. On the other side of town was the woman she was certain was Rob's sister. "I didn't believe the story of the missing birth certificate, especially when Delia said they moved frequently." Anne frowned, wondering what words she could use to tell Rob about Delia. "Maybe I'm being suspicious, but it seems to me that Rob's aunt wanted to pretend the child was hers, and she was taking every possible precaution to destroy proof that Delia was adopted. Why else would they change her name and then move away from the community where everyone knew of the adoption?"

"It seems logical." Susannah held out the sketch. "What do you think?"

Anne studied the drawing, marveling at the resemblance to Rob. "You've captured her perfectly." Surely this was Rob's sister. "I had hoped Delia would remember something. Without that, this is another dead end."

"Delia was only two when her parents died," Susannah reminded Anne. "It's unlikely she'd remember them."

Though Susannah was right, Anne didn't want to admit it. "I hope this isn't simply wishful thinking on my part. For Rob's sake, I hope Delia really is Edith."

Susannah studied Anne's face as carefully as she had Delia Webster's. She was silent for a long moment before she asked, "You love him, don't you?"

"Yes." There was no point in denying it. Anne had admitted the truth to herself. She might as well admit it to her sister-in-law. "The problem is, Rob doesn't feel the same way."

Susannah's eyes darkened and she raised an eyebrow. "Are you certain?"

Though it hurt more than she would have

dreamed possible, Anne nodded. "He could not have made his feelings more clear."

"I'm glad to see you, Miss Anne." Luke grinned when Anne entered the workshop. Though she had expected Rob to be there, only Luke was working, painting details on one of the chariots. Anne tried to bite back her disappointment. She wanted — she needed — to see Rob. That need was so urgent that she had not bothered to change out of her traveling clothes, but had come directly to the converted stable as soon as she had arrived home. But Rob wasn't here.

Luke's grin widened. "Mark and me hoped you'd be back before we left so we could say a proper good-bye."

Good-bye? Anne stared at Luke, trying to make sense of his words. They had a whole other carousel, the one for the man in New York, to create before there was any reason to leave. But something had obviously changed in the two days she had been gone. That something was not good. "Where are you going?" Thank goodness her voice sounded normal. The truth was, she wanted to scream the words.

Oblivious to Anne's distress, Luke grinned again. "Rob's been offered a job as head carver at some new carousel factory near

Lake Ontario." Anne tried not to grimace. This was worse than she had feared, for Lake Ontario was at the other end of the state. Once Rob left, she would never see him again. "We're leaving as soon as this merry-go-round is done," Luke continued. And, judging from the progress the men had made in just a few days, that would be soon. "I reckon we're gonna carve the New York ponies at the factory."

"I guess that's good for you." The manners her mother had instilled in her dictated that Anne say something polite, but what she really wanted to do was find Rob and demand to know why he hadn't told her about the job at the new carousel factory. The answer, Anne suspected, was one she wouldn't like. Rob hadn't told her because she wasn't important to him.

"It's steady work," Luke agreed. " 'Course, Mark's madder than a wet hornet. He's got himself a girl he's sparking, and he doesn't want to leave her."

Whereas Rob had no reason to stay. Anne took a deep breath, trying to quell her disappointment. What had she expected? She had known Rob would leave Hidden Falls. He had told her that. She simply hadn't thought it would be this soon.

"When Rob comes back, would you tell

him I'd like to see him?" Anne clenched her fists, reminding herself that how she felt wasn't important. What mattered was telling Rob about Delia, the woman who might be his sister.

She wanted to see him. Anticipation mingled with dread as Rob followed Mrs. Enke's directions. Anne was back from Saratoga. That was good news. He'd be able to see her at least once more before he left Hidden Falls forever. That was also good news. But what if the reason she wanted to see him was to announce her marriage? The very thought of Anne and Philip together made Rob's stomach clench with pain and slowed his steps. He didn't want to hear that. Indeed, he did not.

"Luke said you were looking for me." As he entered the small office, Rob saw that Anne was sitting behind the desk, both hands in front of her. He looked once, then again, ensuring that his eyes hadn't deceived him. It was true. She wasn't wearing a wedding ring! Rob's spirits began to soar. No matter what she wanted to tell him, at least it wasn't that.

As Anne motioned him to a chair on the opposite side of the desk, the hackles on the back of Rob's neck began to rise. Something was wrong. Not only had she not greeted him with her usual warm smile, but it was also apparent that for some reason, Anne wanted this to be a formal meeting. Why else would she have chosen the office? Why else would she remain behind the desk? Although they had discussed his business on a number of occasions, those discussions had always been informal, the two of them sitting on the patio or gathered around the table in the workshop. This was different, and though Rob didn't know why, his instincts shouted that the reason could not be good.

"I wanted to tell you about my trip to Saratoga." It wasn't simply the setting that was different. So, too, was Anne's voice. Today it was flat, almost cold. Rob had never heard her sound that way. He'd seen her happy, sad, occasionally angry, but he'd never seen this impassivity. Rob wanted to lean forward, to touch Anne's hands and ask her what was wrong. But he couldn't, and so he remained sitting perfectly upright, waiting for whatever it was she wanted to say. It wouldn't be good. He knew that, and so he braced himself for her words.

"I may have found your sister."

Anne continued speaking. Rob heard the sound of her voice, but the words refused to register. He felt the blood drain from his face, and for a second the world turned black. *What had she said?* Rob blinked rapidly, trying to convince himself that he had heard her words correctly. *There was something about Saratoga.* "You went to Saratoga to find Edith?" Rob stared at the woman on the other side of the desk. He had thought he knew Anne Moreland, but he hadn't. Never had he dreamed that she would have done such a thing for him.

Anne nodded. "I didn't want to tell you why we were going in case it turned out to be another dead end."

As she explained why she thought the woman who was now called Delia was his sister, Rob heart beat a tattoo. Was it only yesterday that he had accepted the possibility that he would never find Edith? And now this woman, this wonderful woman, had given him hope. Though she had no reason to care about his missing sister, she did. And Anne had done more than he had. She hadn't merely written letters. She had journeyed to another town to see the woman she believed was Edith. Rob swallowed again, trying to clear his throat. Was it possible? Were the years of searching almost over?

"Susannah made a sketch for you." As

Anne slid the piece of paper across the desk, the last piece of the puzzle slipped into place. The reason for Anne's trip to Saratoga was clear, as was the reason why she had asked Susannah, the artist, to accompany her rather than her twin.

With hands that were remarkably steady, Rob reached for the sheet of paper. He stared at the penciled drawing for a long moment, and as he did his hope turned to certainty. "She's Edith. I know it. This woman looks just like my mother." Rob's heart was pounding so loudly he was certain Anne must hear it. Was there ever such a perfect day? After all those years of dead ends, he was close to being reunited with his sister.

He wanted to shout with sheer joy, but he couldn't — not with Anne sitting there, so prim and proper. Though the woman behind the desk looked like the Anne he knew, Rob had never seen her face so expressionless. She had given him the most wonderful gift of his life, and yet it seemed to mean nothing to her.

"Did something else happen in Saratoga?" There must be a reason for the change.

Anne shook her head. When she spoke, her voice was still as cool as if Rob were a total stranger. "You'll have to convince her.

Delia thinks she's the Barclays' only child."

Barclay. Rob frowned. His aunt and uncle's name was Barton. His sister had been called Edith, not Delia. Though Anne had told him her theory about why Aunt Agnes might have changed his sister's first name, that didn't explain the difference in surnames. Was it possible that there were two women of the right age who looked so much alike? Rob didn't want to believe it.

"I'm going to Saratoga." His sister was there, and maybe — just maybe — he would discover what had caused the change in Anne. Rob looked at the sketch that lay before him, marveling at the effort Anne had taken to help him, unable to reconcile that evidence of caring with the solemn woman on the other side of the desk. "Anne, I told you I needed a miracle, and you gave me one. I don't know how to thank you for everything you've done."

For the first time since he'd entered the room, Rob saw emotion in Anne's eyes. Surely it was his imagination that that emotion was pain. "There's no need for thanks. What I did was nothing more than any friend would do."

Friends. Of course. Rob tried not to frown.

■ ■ ■ ■

He was gone. She'd known that he would take the first train to Saratoga. She would have done the same. Anne closed the book that she had been trying to read. It was useless. Though she turned pages, not a single word was registering. All she saw was Rob's face when she'd told him about Delia. He'd looked so carefree, so happy. For the first time, the lines that had seemed permanently etched between his eyes disappeared. Her heart pounded at the thought that she had helped erase those lines. That was what she wanted, to make Rob happy, and she had done it.

For once, she had not failed. She had been wrong in trying to help Rob establish his own company; he'd made that clear. She'd been wrong in thinking he might care for her as more than a friend. But she had not been wrong in trying to find his sister. If Delia was Edith — and Anne believed she was — Rob's dream of being reunited with his sister would come true.

She had succeeded at something. Why, then, did she feel so sad? It wasn't difficult to find the reason. Rob was gone. This was a short trip, but Anne knew it was only a precursor. Soon he would be gone forever.

She rose and walked toward the door. Though the thought filled her with anguish, she had to accept the fact that Rob would leave her life as easily as he had insinuated his way into it. She wandered around the first floor. Jane was paying visits; Mrs. Enke was taking an afternoon nap. There was no one for Anne to talk to, no one to help dispel the melancholy that came whenever she thought of Rob leaving Hidden Falls. Today the melancholy was deeper than normal, and not even the memory of Rob's happiness diluted it.

Anne climbed the stairs, fully intending to go to her own room. But when she reached the landing, her feet turned right instead of left. Her eyes widened as she realized what she had done. She could turn around. Perhaps she should. But something compelled her to keep walking, to enter the wing that had once been her parents' private domain. Though Dr. Kellogg had told her there was nothing she could have done, his reassurance had not assuaged the sorrow that gripped Anne's heart when she thought of that night.

The hallway looked different than it had the last time she had been there. It was midday now, not night. The smoke had long since dissipated, allowing Anne to view what she had been unable to see that night: the singed wallpaper, the charred pieces of furniture. But, though more than a year had passed, the acrid smell of smoke remained, a pungent reminder of a night none of the Morelands would ever forget.

Anne walked slowly along the hallway, remembering how fear had propelled her that night, how she had run but had felt she was coming no closer, no matter how many steps she took. The door to her parents' chamber hung ajar. Her hand trembling, Anne pushed it open and stared at the room that had figured in her nightmares so many times. There was almost nothing left. The fire had burned hottest here, consuming the draperies and the softer pieces of furniture. Her mother's prized Persian rug and the oil painting her father had commissioned for their tenth anniversary were gone. Someone had even swept away the ashes.

Though her heart pounded with dread, Anne forced herself to look at the bed. It had once boasted a lace canopy and an intricately carved headboard. Now all that remained were four charred posts. Anne closed her eyes for a second, remembering how she had crawled across the floor to reach her parents, remembering her mother's weight as she had dragged her toward the French door, remembering how she had tugged on her father, urging him to move.

And then her thoughts rolled back in time and she remembered her father saying, "All anyone can ask is that you do your very best." How often had he told his children that? When one of them had been discouraged that something they had attempted hadn't been perfect, Papa had helped assuage bruised pride with his words. Anne's lips began to curve as she recalled Papa's smiles.

She touched one of the posts, remembering the costly lace spread that had once covered the bed and the day she had asked her mother if it was a treasure. Mama had shaken her head. "Do you know what the greatest treasure on earth is?" she had asked Anne. "It's happiness, Anne. That's what your father and I wish for you and Jane and Charles."

As the memory of her parents' words flooded through her, Anne felt as if an enormous weight had been lifted from her shoulders. She touched the charred bed once more, then nodded slowly as her heart accepted what her mind already knew. She couldn't have saved her parents' lives. By the time she had reached their room, it was too late. But she had done what her father would have expected; she had done her best. Now it was time to follow her mother's advice and search for the treasure her parents had wished for her.

Anne closed the door softly, knowing she would not return, knowing too that the nightmares were over.

CHAPTER TWELVE

She's Edith. She's my sister. The words reverberated in Rob's mind, keeping time with the clacking of the train wheels. He checked his watch for what had to be the hundredth time. Would this journey never end? Surely it had already lasted a lifetime. When at last the train stopped in Saratoga, he hurried down the steps and followed the directions Anne had given him. He would worry about finding a hotel room later. Now all that mattered was seeing Edith.

Though his heart was pounding louder than the looms in Charles's mill, Rob knocked on the door to the small house, then waited for what felt like another lifetime until it opened.

"What can I do for you?" the man that Rob knew must be Harold Webster asked. Then before Rob could answer, the man's eyes widened. "You look like my wife!"

Harold Webster filled the doorway, blocking the view of the interior. He could not, however, block the sound of a woman's voice. "Sweetheart, who's there?" It was Edith. Of course it was Edith. Rob's heart continued to pound, echoing his thoughts. *Close. I'm so close.*

"Delia, I think you'd better come here." Harold Webster ushered Rob into the small house. Anne had told him it was a comfortable home. If his life had depended on it, Rob couldn't have described a single feature. All he knew was that soon he would see his sister. There was the sound of footsteps on the wooden floor, and then she stood before him. Rob's mouth dropped in surprise. Why hadn't Anne warned him? The woman's face looked exactly like the sketch Susannah had done, but Anne hadn't told him that his sister was about to have a child. The pounding of his heart became a roar in his ears. This was much more than he had expected. A sister plus a niece or nephew. Rob had lived alone for so long that he could hardly believe he might have a family — a real family.

"Oh!" Edith's eyes widened when she saw him, and she leaned against her husband, obviously seeking support. Rob wasn't sure why. Anne had told Edith about him. Was it simply that their resemblance was greater than she had expected?

There was a moment of awkward silence before Harold led the way to a small sofa and helped his wife settle herself there. Though Rob wanted to ask the woman if she remembered anything at all that would prove she was his sister, he hesitated, afraid of the answer.

"You must be Rob Ludlow." Edith's eyes clouded with confusion. "I don't know how to explain the resemblance." She touched the corner of one eye and the cleft in her chin. "We look so much alike, but I have no siblings."

She was his sister. Rob was positive of that. He saw himself in her every gesture. It wasn't coincidence. It was heredity. All he needed was to convince her, but that, Rob suspected, would not be easy. "Are you certain, Mrs. Webster? You were so young when we were parted."

Her hand tightened on her husband's as she gave him a beseeching look. "The resemblance between you and my wife is remarkable," Harold Webster said, "but Delia is an only child."

That was a lie. Rob was as certain of that as he was that he was born to carve carousel horses. "Isn't it possible that your parents hid the truth from you?"

Edith shook her head vehemently. "Why would they do that? They loved me. They were the kindest, most wonderful parents on earth." Rob said a silent prayer of thanksgiving that his fears for his sister's safety had been unfounded. Even though his aunt had once been cruel to him, it appeared that Edith had been showered with kindness.

"No one could have asked for better parents than Agnes and Emil Barclay. If influenza hadn't taken them, I'd probably still be living with them."

Anne had told Rob that Delia's name was Barclay, but she hadn't said that her parents were Agnes and Emil. His aunt and uncle had been Agnes and Emil Barton. Rob took a deep breath as another piece of the puzzle fell into place. The names weren't coincidence any more than the loss of Edith's birth certificate had been coincidence. His aunt and uncle hadn't wanted to be found. That was why they had moved so often and had changed their last name. It would have been too difficult for them to remember to answer to a different name, and so they had kept their first names the same. Changing Edith to Delia would have been simpler because of her age. At two she was young enough to forget that she had ever been called by a different name.

Rob leaned back, relaxing for the first time since he had left Hidden Falls. It all made sense. Delia was Edith. He had found his sister and he had seen that she was happy. If their reunion wasn't the way Rob had envisioned it, he would have to accept it. Though he was convinced this was his sister, without proof, Edith would not believe he was her brother. And proof was one thing Rob did not have.

"I won't trouble you any longer," he said, rising and heading toward the door. It would have to be enough, knowing that Edith was alive and well.

Rob had his hand on the doorknob when a memory assailed him. Turning back to face Edith he asked, "Do you have a jagged scar on your right forearm?"

His sister and her husband exchanged looks of shock.

"How did you know?" Edith looked at her arms, covered with long sleeves, as they had been the day Anne and Susannah had visited her. Rob had seen the sleeves in Susannah's sketch.

Memories of a day he'd almost forgotten flooded back. "When my sister was learning to walk, she fell against the andirons and cut her arm." Rob remembered her screams of pain and their mother's frightened expression. "The wound never healed properly."

Harold nodded toward the chair Rob had just vacated. "You'd better sit down, sir. You and your sister have a lot to talk about."

They talked until late that night and then again in the morning before Rob's train left, recounting stories of their lives, sharing their hopes and fears and dreams. As he walked back to the train station, though the day was damp and dismal, Rob was smiling. He'd found his sister, and she was happy. The worries that had plagued him for so long were gone, replaced with the knowledge that Edith — he couldn't think of her as Delia — was married to a man who obviously loved her. They had agreed that they would stay in touch now that they'd found each other. Perhaps he would even see his nieces and nephews one day. The dead ends were gone.

Rob climbed into the train car and took a window seat. So much had changed in less than a day. Yesterday at this time, he hadn't been certain that his sister was still alive. Now he had met her. Yesterday the most important thing in his life had been finding Edith. Now he had accomplished that mission. Yesterday he had worried that his sister was not happy. Now he knew that she was happier than he'd dreamed possible.

Edith was happy. He was not.

Edith had taken chances. He had not.

Rob stared at the countryside, paying no attention to the vibrant fall colors. Instead, he pictured a beautiful blond woman with a smile that never quite lost the hint of sorrow. He loved Anne Moreland, and the most important thing to him was that she was happy. If that was true, and it was, why hadn't he done more? Rob closed his eyes for a second, admitting his failure. Unlike his sister, he had been afraid to take chances, to try to erase the sorrow. And because he hadn't taken chances, because he hadn't told Anne how he felt, he had added to her sorrow. But that was yesterday. Today would be different.

When she woke, her head was throbbing with pain. Anne moaned softly as she forced her eyes open. She shouldn't have a headache. Normally those were the aftermath of her nightmares, but last night's sleep had been undisturbed. She had had no nightmares, not even any dreams that she recalled, yet her head ached and she was filled with an inexplicable sense of dread. Perhaps it had something to do with the changing seasons. The doctor in Switzerland had told her she might experience facial pain when the weather changed. It must be that.

Belting her wrapper, Anne descended the stairs and padded into the kitchen. Maybe something good could result from her headache. "There's no need to cook dinner today," she told Mrs. Enke. Though she would use her headache as an excuse, the truth was that Anne was concerned about her housekeeper and was constantly searching for ways to help her slow down. "Jane will be out, and I . . ."

Before she could complete the sentence, the older woman rushed to her side and placed a cool hand on her forehead. "Oh, lambie, you're not well."

"It's nothing serious," Anne assured her. "I'll feel better if I rest."

Mrs. Enke clucked, a sure sign that she was worried. "You climb back into that bed of yours, and I'll bring you some dry toast and some of my special chamomile tea. That'll cure what ails you."

Though Anne did not doubt the restorative powers of Mrs. Enke's teas, she doubted that even chamomile would dispel her uneasiness. She felt as if a storm was imminent, yet the sky was clear and the air bore none of the heaviness that normally presaged storms.

"Thank you." She acceded to the older woman's plan but added, "Once you've made the tea, I'd like you to take the rest of the day off. I know you want to visit your cousin." Anne glanced at the kitchen clock. If Mrs. Enke hurried, she could catch the mid-morning train and be at her cousin's house before noon. Though it took a few minutes to override the other woman's protests, Anne finally convinced her.

Whether it was the therapeutic effects of chamomile tea and toast or simply the passage of time, Anne didn't know. What she did know was that by late morning she felt well enough to be out of bed. Her head no longer ached, though she was unable to quell the sense of impending doom. It made no sense. Unless it was the weather, Anne could find no reason why she should feel this way. She was no longer haunted by the fire. The process had been gradual, with yesterday's visit to her parents' room as the culmination. She had faced the demons of her memories and had walked away the victor. The enormous weight of guilt had been lifted and the healing that Dr. Kellogg had predicted had begun.

At one point Anne had worried about her nursery, but there was no longer any need to be concerned. The nursery was successful. Even Charles admitted that the mill workers were more productive now that they didn't worry about their youngest children. Though she had worried about her family, Charles was happier than she had ever seen him, visibly in love with Susannah and eager to become a father. Jane was still a puzzle, but Anne knew she wasn't the cause of her malaise.

That left only Rob. Anne sank into her favorite chair. She didn't want to think about Rob, because that brought pain and did not explain this odd sense of doom. But thoughts of Rob would not be denied. They flooded through her when least expected and they remained, hovering on the fringes of her consciousness. Rob was leaving. Anne drew a deep breath, trying to force back the pain. It hurt to know that Rob would leave and she would never see him again!

Anne clenched the chair arms, her knuckles whitening from the force of her grip. Not even the pain she had endured from her burns could compare to this. That pain was external. This was lodged inside her. She had known that the other pain would diminish with time. This would not. Once Rob was gone, the void inside her would grow, becoming stronger and deeper until it consumed her, leaving little more than an empty shell.

Anne heard the chime of the grandfather clock and the church bells inviting the townspeople to worship. Ordinary sounds on an ordinary Sunday. It was only Anne whose mood was out of the ordinary. Why had no one told her that love could hurt?

She hadn't meant to fall in love with Rob. That wasn't part of her plan, but Mama had told her that love didn't always strike like lightning. Sometimes it grew from the tiniest of seeds, sprouting and blossoming before you recognized it. That was what had happened to Anne. Perhaps it had started at the train station the day she returned when she had wanted to protect Rob from Jane's uncharacteristic rudeness. Perhaps it was later that day when she had seen the magnificent horses he had created. Anne didn't know. All she knew was that she hadn't been honest with herself, with Susannah, and most of all with Rob. She had called what she felt for him friendship when it was really love. The reason wasn't hard to find. Anne was afraid of love. She was afraid she'd fail at love as she'd failed at so many other things. She was afraid Rob would reject her love as he had rejected her dreams for Ludlow Carousels. And because she was afraid, she had not told him of her feelings. It was time to change.

Anne rose, straightening her shoulders and holding her head high. Ever since the fire she had lived in fear, letting those fears control her. She would do that no longer. Though the fears might remain, she would overcome them. Rob had once told her she was courageous. Now was the time to demonstrate that courage. No matter how difficult it might be, she would take the risk. She would follow her father's admonitions and do the best she could as she searched for the treasure of happiness. When Rob returned, Anne would open her heart to him and tell him she loved him. That was the only way she knew to stop the pain. And maybe by then this inexplicable sense of doom would have dissipated.

Anne sniffed. Her room smelled musty. Perhaps that was contributing to her mood. She walked briskly to the window, raised the sash and breathed deeply. She had expected fresh autumn air; instead she smelled smoke. The dread that had clung to her all morning intensified. Instinctively Anne knew this was not an innocent fire. Smoke was drifting around the corner of the house. That meant . . . *No! It couldn't be!* It was. The workshop was on fire. Anne's heart pounded with the realization that there was no one there to battle it. Rob's horses, those incredibly beautiful horses, were in danger.

She raced down the stairs, grabbing the phone. *Answer it! Answer it!* Anne pleaded silently. But there was no answer at Charles and Susannah's house or the Harrods'. It was Sunday morning, and everyone was gone. Anne was alone with the fire.

Oh, no! Not again! Fear poured through her veins as she remembered the crackle of flames, the sting of flying embers, the stench of smoke, the year of unending pain. She couldn't do it. She couldn't go into another burning room. She would fail again as she had failed that night. She had no hoses, no large buckets, nothing that she could use to extinguish the fire. Anne bit back a sob. It was hopeless. Help would not arrive in time to save the workshop. Lillian and the other horses would be lost. There was nothing she could do.

She stood for a moment, paralyzed by fear. Then she shook her head. There was something she could do. Anne took a deep breath and ran to the kitchen. She would not let fire consume Rob's best work. Grabbing a towel, she soaked it in water, then tied it around her face. She laid a second dripping towel over her arm. She could do this. Yes, she could. Resolutely she raced across the lawn to the burning workshop and flung open the door. She would not fail.

It was different this time. The smoke was not as thick; there was more light; Anne was better prepared. This time she knew what to expect. She knew the kind of enemy fire could be, and she was determined to defeat it.

Though Anne closed her eyes until they were mere slits, tears began to pour from them when she entered the smoke-filled room. She took a shallow breath as she oriented herself. Lillian. She had to find Lillian. The stairs to the loft were gone, and flames were feeding on the center table. There was no hope of saving the chariots Mark and Luke had so carefully crafted. Moving as quickly as she dared, Anne reached Lillian. Thank goodness the fire had not yet reached this corner. She threw the second damp towel over the horse's head, then wrapped her arms around its neck, lifting it off the platform. Even though it was a miniature horse, it was heavier than she had expected. It wasn't as heavy as Papa, Anne reminded herself. She had been able to move him.

Another foot. She could carry Lillian

another foot. Though it felt as if she had been inside the burning workshop for hours, at last she reached the door. Ignoring the way her arms ached, Anne pulled the painted pony outside, stopping for a deep breath only when Lillian was a safe distance from the workshop. Five more. She could do it. She could save Rob's horses. Anne ran back. In the distance, she heard the train whistle and the church bells. Four more. With each minute, the fire intensified, the flames lapping more of the dried wood, charring whitewashed timbers. Three more. The towels had dried and provided little protection. She should return to the house and soak them again. No time. Two more. Anne heard the ominous creak of the rafters. One more.

Rob couldn't contain his grin as the train pulled into the station. He was home. Odd how he'd never thought of Hidden Falls that way. Though he'd been here six months, he hadn't let himself put down roots. He had known from the beginning that this was a temporary stop, the first of many. But now, maybe that wouldn't be the case. Maybe Hidden Falls could be his home. His and Anne's.

He was smiling as he descended the iron

steps, his eyes drawn to the hill. In just a few minutes, he'd see Anne again and he'd know if there was a chance that his dreams could come true. Maybe, just maybe . . .

Rob's smile faded and he felt the blood drain from his face. Trees blocked the view of the houses, but nothing could hide the billows of ominous black smoke that rose from the center house. Fairlawn was on fire! For a second Rob was unable to move. How much bad luck could one family endure? At least they were all gone. Or were they?

The dread that swept through Rob threatened to buckle his knees. *Anne!* What if Anne was there? Rob looked around. Where were the wagons when you needed them? No one had come to greet this train, and the streets were empty. There was only one way to reach Fairlawn. Rob started to run. Would he be in time? He had to be. That thought propelled his feet. His side ached, his legs felt as if they were on fire, and his breaths were coming in short painful pants. He had to get there. He had to find Anne. He couldn't lose her. As he reached the crest of the hill, Rob's panic lessened. He was past the trees now and could see that the smoke was coming from the workshop. Anne was safe. Thank goodness! His horses could be replaced; the woman he loved could not.

But still Rob ran, driven by a force he could not explain. He had to reach the fire. He had to extinguish it. He cut through the yard, catching his sleeve on one of the overgrown rosebushes. And then he saw it. Though the smoke was thick and acrid, Rob could distinguish the outline of a figure inside the former stable. Someone was in the workshop. Who could be so foolish? Fear took his breath as surely as exertion had, but his legs redoubled their efforts, and Rob sprinted the last few yards, desperate to reach the workshop. Though his heart pounded, filling his head with the sound of rushing blood, he heard the ominous crack and knew that the roof was close to collapsing. He had to get there. Now!

The doorway darkened and the figure emerged. It was a woman. Rob saw the long skirts. She was dragging something. His eyes widened in alarm as he recognized both the woman and the object. It couldn't be. It wasn't possible. Stunned, Rob realized that his eyes had not lied. Anne was carrying one of his horses. How on earth? Why on earth? As the questions barreled through him, he reached Anne and pulled the horse away from her.

"No!" she cried, her voice muffled by the

towel she had wrapped around her face. "Further." She gestured toward the house, and Rob saw the other horses lying on their sides next to Fairlawn. This wasn't her first trip into the inferno.

"Run!" he cried as he heard a beam snap. Grabbing the horse that this crazy, foolish, wonderful woman had risked her life to save, he followed Anne to safety. As they stood there, panting from exertion and relief, Rob looked at the woman he loved. Her clothing was blacked with soot, her face streaked with ashes, her hair darkened by the dirt. He was certain she had never looked more beautiful.

"Thank God you're safe!" Gently, he brushed the singed hair from Anne's face, his heart pounding with relief and awe. "What on earth possessed you to go in there?" He knew how terrified Anne was of the smallest flame, and yet she had gone into a burning building. Rob led her to one of the garden benches, wrapping his arms around her waist. There was nothing he could do to save the workshop, and the ground was so wet from last night's rain that there appeared no danger of the fire spreading. All that mattered now was Anne.

Though she was trembling from the aftermath of her ordeal, her eyes were clear as she faced him. "I had to save your horses. I couldn't let the fire destroy them." The words were simple. The act she described was not.

Rob took a deep breath and tried to tamp back his anger. "You risked your life for pieces of painted wood?" Though his voice was harsher than he'd intended, he couldn't control it. He was quaking from the realization of how close he had come to losing Anne.

She shook her head slowly and looked at the horses lying on their sides. Like her, they were streaked with soot. Rob suspected they would need to be repainted. "They're not just paint and wood, Rob." Anne's voice was low and intense. "They're your life's work. You said yourself that they were the best you've ever done."

Rob wasn't certain which emotion was stronger: anger that she had been so foolish or awe that she had faced her worst nightmare for him. "The horses could be replaced. You can't." He put his hand under Anne's chin and tipped it so that he could look into her eyes. "I can carve another horse, but I could never, ever find another woman I love as much as you."

Though her face was covered with soot, Anne's eyes shone brightly. "You love me?"

There was a hint of wonder in her voice, as if his declaration had surprised her. Rob nodded slowly. While this wasn't the way he had planned it, he had to continue. He couldn't let this incredibly courageous woman slip out of his life. If she could face the fire, he could face the possibility of rejection. His heart pounded at the realization of all she had risked for him. Surely that was proof that she regarded him as more than a friend.

"My darling Anne, I've been such a fool. Yes, I love you. I think I started loving you even before we met." He brushed a piece of soot from her eyelashes. "Charles's stories made me realize that you were strong and courageous as well as beautiful."

"But I'm not beautiful. I have scars."

The uncertainty on her face told Rob she thought he was simply being polite. "You are beautiful, Anne, inside and out. I love that, but it's only one of the things I love about you." He smiled at her, hoping she would believe him. Everything important in his life depended on that. "I love you more than I ever dreamed it possible to love a person. I love you so much that my heart aches when we're apart, but — like a fool — I didn't tell you."

The woman Rob loved so dearly smiled at

him, the expression in her eyes filling his heart with hope that she believed him and that by some miracle she loved him too. "Why didn't you say anything?" she asked.

Rob stroked her cheek. "I was afraid to tell you what I felt, because I thought I had nothing to offer you. I can't give you all the things Philip Biddle can. I'll never be able to afford a fancy house or servants. All I can offer you is my heart and the promise that I'll love you every day of my life." He gazed into the eyes that had haunted his dreams, and the emotion he saw there made his heart beat faster. "If you love me half as much as I love you, that will be enough."

For a second Anne was silent, and Rob feared that he had misunderstood. Perhaps she didn't love him. Perhaps what she felt for him was nothing more than friendship. Then Anne smiled. "Love is all I ever wanted or needed. I love you, Rob. So very, very much."

Rob was certain his heart would burst with happiness. The woman he loved was saying the words he longed to hear. *Anne loved him!* He wanted to shout it to the world, but as he opened his mouth to speak, the lump that filled his throat made the words come out as little more than a whisper. "Oh, my love!"

He loved her! Rob loved her! Never before had Anne seen a smile like the one that lit his face. Though it blazed hotter than the fire, its warmth brought healing, not destruction. The emptiness that had been inside her for so long began to disappear, replaced by the love that she saw in Rob's smile.

When he started to speak, Anne laid a finger over his lips. It was her turn. She had to make him understand that the old Anne was gone. "When I came back from Switzerland, I thought I'd be able to resume the life I'd had before the fire. I knew I had changed, but I thought that everything else would be the same as it was before. I was wrong."

Anne placed her hand on Rob's cheek, reveling in the firmness of his skin. He was a good man, an honorable man, and by some miracle, he loved her. "At first I was afraid of the changes until I realized that they are a normal part of life. Charles has Susannah. Jane doesn't need me any more; she's the strong one now. My family has changed, and so have I."

Anne took a deep breath. If they were going to have a future together, and oh! how she hoped they were, it was important that Rob knew what mattered to her. "I don't need a fancy house. I don't even need to live in Hidden Falls. What I need and what I want most is a family of my own." Anne paused and looked up at Rob, hoping he would see the love shining from her eyes. "A family with you."

Rob had been listening silently, the expression in his eyes intensifying with each word she uttered. "Family is important," he said. "From the very beginning, I envied Charles his family. One of the reasons I agreed to make the carousel was that it was for his sister."

Sister. So much had happened in such a short time that Anne had forgotten Rob's trip to Saratoga. "Is Delia your sister?"

He nodded. "Thanks to you, I found her." For a second those beautiful eyes that were so like his sister's clouded. "It was wonderful to see her again, but it wasn't what I had expected. I had thought that when I found Edith we would begin a new life together. Instead, I felt the way I do when I reach the end of a good book. That story was over, and now it's time to start a new one . . . with you."

Rob took both of Anne's hands in his. Though his eyes were serious as he looked down at her, the fires of love shone clearly, warming Anne and filling the last empty space in her heart. "This isn't the way I had planned to ask you, but I can't wait for the perfect time and place." His voice was husky with emotion. "I love you, Anne. Will you make my life complete? Will you be my family? What I'm trying to say is, will you marry me?"

Happiness greater than anything she had ever dreamed washed over her. Anne gazed at the man who loved her despite her imperfections, the man who could turn tears into joy, the only man she would ever love.

"Yes, my dearest, a thousand times yes."

In the distance, church bells rang, marking the end of the service. In a few weeks they would ring again, this time to announce a beginning, the beginning of a new family: hers and Rob's.

Her heart overflowing with love, Anne raised her face for his kiss.

AUTHOR'S LETTER

Dear Reader,

If you've read my earlier books including the *War Brides Trilogy,* you know how much I like creating connected stories. It was that love, combined with an incurable case of carousel fever, that led to the *Hidden Falls Romances.* I knew I couldn't write just one book featuring those wonderful painted ponies, so I created a whole town with secrets to be uncovered and many, many stories to be told.

I hope you enjoyed Anne and Rob's story and that you were intrigued by some of Hidden Falls' other residents. If you wondered what Jane was doing all those times she disappeared and whether she and Matt were really in love, you'll find the answers (and maybe some surprises) in *The Brass Ring,* which will be published in February 2007.

I can also promise you that you haven't seen the last of Bertha, Ralph, Philip and

Brad. And then there are the newcomers, who couldn't resist the town's appeal any more than I could. Like the best of carousels, this is going to be a long ride, and I hope you'll be there with me.

Happy reading!

Amanda Harte

ABOUT THE AUTHOR

A chance encounter with a merry-go-round horse at — of all places — a highway rest area led to **Amanda Harte's** incurable case of carousel fever. She's been planning stories about painted ponies and the people who love them ever since and is delighted to share the first of the Hidden Falls Romances with you.

Amanda is a charter member of Romance Writers of America, co-founder of its New Jersey chapter and an avid traveler. She married her high school sweetheart, who shares her love of travel and who's driven thousands of miles to help her research her books. They've recently fulfilled a long-time dream and are now living in the American West, where they're continuing to search for antique carousels.

Painted Ponies is Amanda's eighth romance novel for AVALON. In addition to her highly acclaimed *War Brides Trilogy* (*Dancing in the Rain, Whistling in the Dark* and *Laughing at the Thunder*), she has written three *Unwanted Legacies* books (*Strings Attached, Imperfect Together* and *Bluebonnet Spring*) as well as *Moonlight Masquerade,* the story of a romance writer with a problem.

Amanda loves hearing from readers and encourages you to visit her Web site at:

www.amandaharte.com.

The employees of Thorndike Press hope you have enjoyed this Large Print book. All our Thorndike, Wheeler, and Kennebec Large Print titles are designed for easy reading, and all our books are made to last. Other Thorndike Press Large Print books are available at your library, through selected bookstores, or directly from us.

For information about titles, please call:
  (800) 223-1244

or visit our Web site at:
  http://gale.cengage.com/thorndike

To share your comments, please write:
  Publisher
  Thorndike Press
  295 Kennedy Memorial Drive
  Waterville, ME 04901